Woman with a Blue Pencil

Also by Gordon McAlpine

Hammett Unwritten (as Owen Fitzstephen)

Woman with a Blue Pencil
A Novel

Gordon McAlpine

SEVENTH STREET BOOKS®
AN IMPRINT OF PROMETHEUS BOOKS
59 JOHN GLENN DRIVE • AMHERST, NY 14228
www.seventhstreetbooks.com

Published 2015 by Seventh Street Books®, an imprint of Prometheus Books

This is a work of fiction. Characters, organizations, products, locales, and events portrayed in this novel either are products of the author's imagination or are used fictitiously.

Cover images: paper © siloto / Shutterstock; scribble © Can Stock Photo, Inc. / maryloo; man © Media Bakery; hand © Babii Nadiia / Shutterstock

Cover design by Jacqueline Nasso Cooke

Inquiries should be addressed to
Seventh Street Books
59 John Glenn Drive
Amherst, New York 14228
VOICE: 716–691–0133
FAX: 716–691–0137
WWW.SEVENTHSTREETBOOKS.COM

19 18 17 16 15   5 4 3 2 1

Library of Congress Cataloging-in-Publication Data

McAlpine, Gordon, author.
    Woman with a blue pencil : a novel / Gordon McAlpine.
        pages cm
    ISBN 978-1-63388-088-7 (paperback) — ISBN 978-1-63388-089-4 (e-book)
    1. Private investigators—Fiction. 2. Murder—Investigation—Fiction.
I. Title.

PS3563.C274W66 2015
813'.54—dc23

2015023614

Printed in the United States of America

To my compañero, Roy Langsdon

December 7, 1941:

353 fighters, bombers, and torpedo planes launched from six aircraft carriers of the Imperial Japanese Navy attack without warning the American naval base at Pearl Harbor, Hawaii, killing over 2,400 Americans, decimating the US Pacific fleet, and instigating America's entrance to the Second World War.

February 19, 1942:

Executive Order 9066 authorizes local American military commanders to designate "exclusion zones," in the USA from which "any or all persons may be excluded." Along the Pacific coast, this results in the relocation to internment camps of 110,000 people of Japanese heritage, most US citizens.

August 30, 2014:

A dusty lockbox is found and removed from the attic of a house scheduled for demolition in Garden Grove, California. Inside the lockbox are three items. The first is a pulp spy thriller published in 1945 under the pen name William Thorne. The second is a sheaf of letters from the book's editor, primarily addressed to its author, dating from 1941–1944. The last is an unpublished novella handwritten by the same author on 102 sheets of WWII-era, GI-issue writing paper, mud-splattered and bloodied in some spots. It is signed with the author's real name, Takumi Sato, and is titled "The Revised."

THE REVISED—CHAPTER ONE

By Takumi Sato

> *. . . he'll never understand the nature of his sudden alienation, because he's never known that he is a fictional character. He still doesn't know. So how can he grasp what's happened to him, that he's been cut from a novel-in-progress, excised from his world, which from this point forward carries on around him even though it contains neither memory nor record of his ever having existed? In short, how can he understand that he is the abandoned creation of a conflicted author, whose tossing of typewritten pages into a trash can has not snuffed out everything and everyone written on them?*
>
> —Aldous Huxley, overheard in conversation
> at Clifton's Cafeteria, Los Angeles

On the evening of December 6, 1941, Sam Sumida shifted in his seat at the crowded Rialto Movie House in downtown Los Angeles. It was about a third of the way into the new picture, *The Maltese Falcon*, and on screen Humphrey Bogart knocked the gun from Peter Lorre's hand and began slapping the smaller man silly. Sumida knew the scene was coming. He'd read the novel. In the past weeks, he'd read everything Hammett had ever written, having concluded, after a short period of research, that no other writer possessed either the background or the willingness to depict the PI business realistically. And, since the unsolved murder of Sumida's wife, Kyoko, eleven months before, it had

9

become critical to him that he discern *some* source from which to draw instruction in the art of detection. (All those How-to-be-a-Private-Eye primers had proved little more useful as practical manuals than the outdated, sanitized crime fantasies of S. S. Van Dine or the absurdly plotted puzzles of those famous lady-novelists from England.)

Hammett told it straight, Sumida believed.

And he needed some straight instruction. A PhD in Oriental Art History, which, until recently, he'd taught as a part-time instructor at three local colleges, hardly prepared him for work as a gumshoe. Before that, his mother and father, who'd emigrated from Nagasaki to Long Beach a year before he was born, had raised him to rely on modesty rather than bravado to get by in the white man's world. This had worked well enough for the first thirty years of his life. Intelligence, wit, and an instinct for knowing just the right moment to gracefully leave his Caucasian colleagues to their private diversions had resulted in success in the art history field. He'd bought a small house in Echo Park—quite impressive for the son of a fisherman. But then somebody put a .22 slug in his wife's brain and dumped her body into the harbor at San Pedro, stumping a disinterested LAPD in the process. So, now, Sumida, who'd come alone to the Rialto, watched Humphrey Bogart with a concentrated attention unlike that of others in the Saturday night crowd (most of whom were here either on dates or as respite from an afternoon spent shopping in the nearby garment or jewelry districts, Christmas 1941 being less than three weeks away). Sometimes, Sumida leaned so far forward, unconsciously straining toward the screen, that his face almost brushed against the coiffed head of the woman in the row ahead of his.

In this way, he noted the boldness with which Bogart's Sam Spade put questions to even the most formidable adversaries ... the heedless way Spade diverted questions when they were put to him, even by the cops ... Spade's seeming disregard for the possibility of failure. Of course, Sumida knew that studying fictional gumshoes had its limitations. But the cops had never wanted him around and the licensed PIs he'd subsequently hired, who consumed whatever cash he'd managed to save, likewise wanted him out of the way during their futile investigations. So Sam Sumida's opportunities to learn were limited. Now, all that was left to him were fictions. But he did not lack for native intelligence, could converse with almost anyone in a manner simultaneously persistent and polite, was as physically courageous as the next guy, and possessed self-defense skills, developed in boyhood, which far exceeded those of most. Additionally, and most importantly, his motivation was personal.

Still, quitting his teaching positions to devote all his time to investigating Kyoko's murder may have been rash.

His aunt and uncle had told him it had been mad.

But, truly, what else mattered?

Unfortunately, Sumida had made little or no progress in the weeks since he'd taken up the investigation. He'd begun, reasonably enough, by gathering copies of the police report and the scattershot notes from the three PIs he'd hired and fired, settling down for the better part of a weekend with the documents spread on his dining room table like pieces of a jigsaw puzzle. Might he discern a lead among the summarized interviews and scrawled lists detailing Kyoko's routines—a lead that had eluded the professionals? No. There was, of course, the "revelation" that for the final months of her life she had been carrying on an adulterous affair. Sumida had suspected this long before the LAPD confirmed it. Some nights, she hadn't come home at all. So what else was he to think, particularly when she answered his increasingly passionate queries only with stubborn silence? Still, he never stopped loving her.

He hadn't stopped yet.

He knew that for the past few years he'd been distracted with his work, flattered by offers to lecture at various colleges or to publish articles in journals. And he knew Kyoko's life managing a dental office hadn't been nearly so fulfilling for her. Now, he couldn't imagine ever again taking the same egoistic pleasure in career accomplishments, a secondary reason he'd resigned his positions.

Immediately after the crime, the uncovering of her adultery naturally threw suspicion on Sumida (the cuckolded spouse is always the first suspect). But at the time of the murder Sumida had been in Berkeley at the University of California to give a series of visiting lectures on the art of the Edo period. Absent husband, the adulterous lover was next on the list of suspects. Who else had had access and potential motive? It was at this point that the investigations all hit dead ends. Both the police and the PIs got positive identifications of Kyoko from half a dozen hotel desk clerks in downtown LA ("Beautiful Oriental girl with a streak of white in her black hair"), but none of these desk clerks had been able to offer more than a cursory description of the man who'd been with her—just a six foot tall Caucasian of unspecified hair and eye color. The names signed in the hotel registers were always absurd fabrications: "Mr. and Mrs. G. Washington," "Mr. and Mrs. A. Lincoln," etc. Sumida later called again on the hotel desk clerks who'd recognized Kyoko, but he got nothing more from them than had the other investigators (except for admonitions that he should have kept better watch on such a woman). Canvassing additional downtown hotels, as well as inns and motor lodges up and down the coast from Malibu to Laguna Beach, he found no other desk clerks who recognized Kyoko.

Sumida's next stop had been the scene of the crime, San Pedro. A harbor town with a racially mixed population (including many Japanese) and a chip on its shoulder as wide as the blue Pacific. The police report indicated the particular pier against which Kyoko's body had washed up, though exactly where along the harbor she'd been shot and dumped was impossible to figure due to tides and the churning and stirring of so many commercial boats. When Sumida asked locals whether they remembered hearing a gunshot on the night of January 11—almost eleven months before—he was met only with incredulous expressions.

And now, on the big screen at the Rialto, Humphrey Bogart gave the pistol back to Peter Lorre, whom Bogart did not consider formidable enough even to pay the respect of keeping disarmed.

Such sublime confidence . . .

Did Sumida really think he could gain such qualities just from observing a movie detective—even a good one, like Spade?

No.

The truth was he'd come here, in large part, because he simply didn't know what else to do with himself; tonight, the pain of yet another solitary dinner in what had been *their* kitchen had felt too much to bear, almost dangerous.

So this was the first movie he'd allowed himself since Kyoko's murder. The first respite.

The detective-theme alleviated some of his guilt.

But he'd always loved movies of all kinds. Sure, he chose *The Maltese Falcon* because it *might* contain a detail of detective work that could be useful to his investigation. And he may have noted Spade's techniques and mannerisms with more focus than did those around him. Nonetheless, he smiled with the rest of the audience when the ineffectual Peter Lorre aimed his recently returned pistol again at the bigger, tougher man, repeating his original demands. Bogart could disarm Lorre as easily as before, but now the chuckling gumshoe seemed charmed by the audacity of his diminutive opponent. Watching the movie made Sumida almost happy.

Then the black-and-white scene skidded and slipped sideways on the movie screen. For a moment, the sprockets on the film stock became visible, sliding up and off the screen with the last of the black and white images.

The screen became blindingly white. The rat-a-tat-a-tat of the spinning reels in the projectionist's booth replaced the soundtrack.

The film had broken.

The projectionist shut the machine down, casting the theater into darkness.

❧

Excerpt from a letter dated December 10, 1941:

        . . . so, in light of last Sunday's tragic
    events at Pearl Harbor, we must return your
    book proposal and opening chapters. Despite

my initial enthusiasm, its publication is
now impossible. While this is doubtless
disappointing, I feel you cannot be much
surprised. The world has changed. Even Mar-
quand's successful Mr. Moto series is bound
to come to a screeching halt. Nonetheless,
we believe you are a talented writer and we
encourage you to further develop your craft.

Our accounting department will antic-
ipate your immediate return of the $350
advance we sent with our most recent
correspondence.

Sincerely,

Maxine Wakefield
Maxine Wakefield,
Associate Editor,
Metropolitan Modern Mysteries, Inc.

P.S. If you were to consider revising your
work to avoid the obvious issues, which
would include cutting and replacing not
only your Japanese hero Sumida but also
the Caucasian villain, I would be willing
to take a second look. Of course, I understand that this amounts to your writing a
different book. But since you've completed
only three chapters to date, your invest-
ment of time and effort have been rela-
tively small and so re-envisioning may be a
viable option for you, Mr. Sato.

Thinking aloud . . . Perhaps you could
still employ an Oriental as your protagonist, a Korean or Chinese. I don't mean to
offend by suggesting that Oriental races are
in any way interchangeable, but, frankly,

what most fascinated me in your initial submission was the groundbreaking challenge
of pulling off an Oriental protagonist in
a popular genre. After all, as you likely
already know, Earl Der Biggers's Charlie
Chan books do not actually feature Chan as
the protagonist, and the same is true of Mar-
quand's Mr. Moto novels. These books remain
Caucasian-centric, even if the crimes are
ultimately "solved" by the secondary characters, Chan and Moto. So you may still have
the opportunity to break new ground!

Now, even if you were to change your protagonist's nationality, I believe current
events dictate that your new Korean or
Chinese hero be far more American/Apple pie
than your discarded character, the grieving
Nisei academic, Sumida. Actually, you might
even position your new Oriental hero <u>against</u>
Japanese Fifth Columnists. Yes! Patriotism
will sell in the coming period. A spy novel
. . . Just musing here, you understand.
These are <u>your</u> decisions. I would never
tell an author what to write, particularly
a young and talented one just starting
to make his way. However, I want you to
know that if you chose to write something
along the lines I've outlined above, I'd be
delighted to see it and just possibly we'd
be able to work together after all.

Whatever you decide, best of luck.

P.P.S. One last thought is that you'd need
to set the book firmly in our current,
post-Pearl Harbor world to give more immediate context to your new protagonist's
challenges.

☙

Excerpt from chapter one of *The Orchid and the Secret Agent*, a novel by William Thorne
    Metropolitan Modern Mysteries, Inc., New York, N.Y., 1945

. . . Jimmy Park slipped his .45 into one pocket of his raincoat, though he suspected his Taekwondo fighting skills would render use of the weapon unnecessary. Besides, the modus operandi of Jap agents here in Los Angeles tended more toward sneaking and plotting than man-to-man confrontation. They were generally too weak to settle things physically, unlike real Americans. And even when they did put their inferior Karate techniques to use, it still remained all about deception and unruly kicking. Jimmy Park was of Korean ancestry but, having been raised in Glendale, California, among whites, he was as American as they came—with one exception: he had learned Taekwondo at a tiny *dojang* on Brand Boulevard from a *kwan jang nim*, or grandmaster, of Korean fighting. Like Jimmy and his parents, the grandmaster had arrived on these shores before the Oriental Exclusion Act of 1924. Now, Jimmy was nearly a Taekwondo Master himself. Nonetheless, his heroes were American boxers: Jack Dempsey was his favorite. And the Negro Joe Louis also inspired him, as Jimmy was not prejudiced. In any case, his own lightning fast hands and feet had proven more than sufficient on many occasions.

Still, these sneaky Fifth Columnists, who smiled one moment and then stabbed you in the heart the next, *were* dangerous, in the manner of night-crawling scorpions. Their brutal, decades-long occupation of Park's ancestral Korean peninsula was bad enough. But Pearl Harbor truly indicated the Jap nature. A surprise attack . . . Jimmy grieved for all those sailors' bodies entombed in the sunken USS *Arizona*. He wasn't ever going to forget. Or forgive.

He reached for his hat but was interrupted by a familiar rap at the front door of his comfortable Echo Park bungalow. It was Sergeant Joe

Lucas of the LAPD, who often stopped by Jimmy's house on his way home from work to share a snort of his Korean pal's good Templeton rye.

Jimmy Park opened the door.

"What'ya got your coat on for?" the youthful, blue-eyed Lucas asked, stepping past his friend and straight into the house. "You can't go out in this rain now that I'm here for company."

"You're dripping everywhere," Jimmy observed.

"Well, that's what happens when it's raining outside," Joe replied, smiling. "But I figure by about the fourth snort of your good stuff I should be pretty well dried out."

"Yeah, 'drying out' is what you need," Jimmy said. "And I'm not talking about your wet clothes."

"Oh great, now you're sounding like my wife," Joe said.

Jimmy held up his hands. "Hey, I'm not one to lecture you about drinking, pal."

"You got that right," Joe replied.

"But your police skills haven't failed you, Joe," Jimmy retorted, putting his hat on. "I got my coat and hat for a reason."

"You can't go out on a night like this. Besides, it's January 22, 1942. A national holiday."

Jimmy looked at his friend, suspicious. "What holiday?"

Joe widened his eyes as if shocked that Jimmy could be so ignorant. "It's 'Jimmy Stays Home to Drink with his Buddy Joe Night'! Good lord, even the late shifts at the war plants take tonight off to celebrate our good drinking here in your fine home."

Jimmy grinned and pointed to the shelf with the rye and the shot glasses. "You stay, Joe. Have one or two on me. *Mi casa es tu casa.*"

"I don't speak Mexican," Joe replied.

"Just lock up after yourself," Jimmy said.

Joe squinted in confusion. "Wait. What's so pressing that you can't even have one?"

"We got a tip that a Jap agent we've been on the lookout for will be at the Rialto Movie House. When the picture's over, I'll be waiting for him."

"Why don't you just call headquarters?" Joe asked. "Let them throw a dragnet around the place. Or call the Feds."

Jimmy shrugged. "We don't exactly have any evidence on this guy. Not yet. So I'm supposed to make his acquaintance and see if I can get him to give us some."

"The hard way or the soft way?" Joe inquired.

Jimmy Park was valuable to law enforcement agencies not only because of his expertise as a PI but also because of his facility with Oriental languages. Additionally, mild facial scaring and subtle skin discolorations suffered years before in a fire allowed him to pass for either Chinese or Japanese (while barely diminishing his unusually handsome Asian face). Resultantly, he had infiltrated more than one espionage ring even before the events of December 7, 1941, and, since then, he had proven invaluable to the American cause.

But this new case was the most challenging he had faced.

"We'll start with the 'soft' way," he said to his friend. "I'll cozy up to him like I'm just another Jap. But if that doesn't work . . ." He shrugged and patted the raincoat pocket with the .45.

"What can you tell me?"

"Tell you, a lowly sergeant?"

"Ah, go drown yourself in the rain, Jimmy."

Jimmy laughed and patted Joe on the shoulder. "LAPD found a Jap farmer eviscerated in his own bean field out near Carson," he explained.

Joe shrugged as he started for the rye. "So what makes it a Federal case? Couldn't it'a just been a neighbor who'd had his fill of the sneaky bastards? Not that I approve, of course . . ."

"A source I can't name believes the farmer may have been involved with a Jap spy ring that stretches from south of the Mexican border all the way up to Seattle."

"So who knocked him off?" Joe asked, taking hold of the bottle. "One of ours?"

Jimmy shook his head. "The spy ring employs a formidable assassin, who, as yet, we've been unable to identify. A Jap, of course. Reputedly possessed of 'ninja' skills. Vicious people . . ."

"Why would they knock him off?"

"We don't know. But there's reason to believe he was unwilling to go along with the organization's nefarious plans to strike against America. In the end, he must have had a conscience. Not all Japs are bad."

Joe poured the rye into a shot glass. "And the agent at the Rialto tonight . . . Is he there to make a hit?"

"We don't know that either."

"You need a better inside man," Joe observed, throwing back the first shot of rye.

"Yeah, that's what the Feds think too," Jimmy answered. "That's why . . ." He stopped.

Joe looked at his friend. "You, Jimmy?"

"Can't comment on that, pal."

Joe grinned and patted Jimmy on the shoulder. "So, how'll you pick this assassin out of the exiting crowd, since he ain't going to be wearing no ninja costume?"

"How many Japs do you think are going to the movies these days?"

"Then get your backside out of here, Jimmy," Joe said, toasting him farewell. "And don't worry. I'll turn out the lights and lock up after myself. And I'll leave a nip in the bottle for you."

"Yeah, you do that," Jimmy answered with a grin as he closed the front door, racing in the rain across his small lawn to his car, a '37 Dodge Coupe.

❧

THE REVISED—CHAPTER ONE cont'd.

Sumida sighed and settled back in his seat in the darkened Rialto Movie House, expecting the house lights to rise for a minute or two before Bogart and the others reappeared in the dangerous mire of Hammett's adventure—just a minute or two, as the projectionist rethreaded his machine. That would be long enough for the Saturday night crowd to turn to one another with quips or questions or observations about the last time they'd been cast so suddenly from the world of a movie back into the humdrum of a mere theater seat.

But none of this happened.

Not even two seconds passed before the projector hummed back to life and the screen was again filled with light and motion.

But the picture did not pick up where it had left off. This happened among inexperienced projectionists. Sometimes they ran the wrong reel. For a moment, Sumida watched, trying to place the action on the screen into the story of *The Maltese Falcon* as he knew it from the book. But this was something different—Katherine Hepburn hit long, arching drives on a golf course while Spencer Tracy observed her affectionately, all as a wry musical score lent the scene an ambiance of humor and romance.

"Hey, what's going on?" Sumida muttered.

"Shhh," responded those seated around him.

"But look, it's Spencer Tracy," he whispered to no one in particular. "What happened to our movie?" he asked, raising his voice.

He expected others to be asking the same question, perhaps even whistling at the screen or up to the projectionist's booth in derision.

"It's *Woman of the Year*," a burly man in the row behind him said, matter-of-factly. "What do you think you been looking at the last half-hour?"

Sumida had never even heard of the movie. "They put on the wrong picture," he said.

"Shush," said a woman seated beside him. "We're trying to watch."

"What happened to *The Maltese Falcon*?" he muttered.

"Just shut up," said the burly man.

Sumida stared at the screen a moment longer. Hepburn and Tracy...

Was this some kind of gag that the whole audience was in on? He didn't get it.

Confused, he settled back in his seat. His natural impulse was to pipe down, to watch this new movie to its end and then, perhaps tomorrow or the next day, to see *The Maltese Falcon* elsewhere. He never courted the attention of strangers, particularly as the confusion he felt now could leave him open to the sort of public humiliation he'd sought to avoid ever since his difficult days as the only Nisei student in his elementary school. Still, he didn't understand why all the others in the audience seemed undisturbed by the switching of the films. But he was a rationalist and assumed it was either an elaborate joke (but how and why?) or someone's simple mistake. If he was being tricked, then his instinct was to deny his tormentors the satisfaction of his showing distress. Or, alternatively, when others made mistakes, Sumida often found himself feeling so embarrassed on their behalf that he'd opt to underestimate or, if possible, deny that any mistake had occurred at all. "No, rye bread is what I ordered," he'd reassure the forgetful deli worker, despite having asked for sourdough.

Either way, staying silent was the most natural strategy for him.

But tonight needed to be different, he thought.

After all, would Sam Spade have remained in *his* seat, watching a movie he hadn't chosen to see? Sumida was embarked on the murder investigation of his wife, for God's sake. What kind of man was he to shrink into the darkened audience now, when the stakes were so low? Besides, he *needed* his questions answered about what had just happened here—why everyone else in the audience seemed satisfied with this "other" movie. A true detective did not let such matters lie, even in his private life.

So he stood and scuttled sideways out of the crowded row.

He'd take this up with the manager.

You don't pay to see one movie and wind up in another. With all the things in life that were beyond one's control, choice of movie ought not to be one. (Kyoko doubtless would have preferred the romantic comedy, but that was neither here nor there, he reminded himself.)

As he started up the aisle, he heard whispers:

"Hey look, is that loudmouth a Jap?" the woman seated in front of him asked, her face illuminated by the light of the film as she turned back.

"What, a dirty Jap?" the burly man who'd sat behind him growled menacingly, staring down his row at Sumida, who'd started up the aisle.

Sumida paused. He had been born at LA County General Hospital, attended public schools, and run the 100 and the 220 on the track team at Long Beach Wilson High School. He didn't have to put up with abuse. But he kept walking, bursting through the double doors and into the lobby.

A teenaged usher, who was leaning over the counter of the snack stand, whispering to the blonde girl who sold candy and pop, turned and looked at Sumida with wide eyes.

"I need to see the manager," Sumida said. "Now."

The usher's Adam's apple moved up and down before he answered. "He's in his office." He pointed to a shadowed corner and up a narrow flight of wooden stairs, which looked like an architectural afterthought in the otherwise plush lobby.

Sumida crossed the lobby and walked up the stairs, stopping at the door. A nameplate read: "Manager," which he reflected could not have inspired much confidence in the otherwise nameless man who came to work each day knowing he could be replaced without his employers even having to change the nameplate. Sumida knocked but didn't wait for an answer before walking in. Bogart wouldn't have waited.

The office had no windows—likely a converted storage room. Movie posters from closed engagements were carelessly taped to the walls (including, strangely, *The Maltese Falcon*).

"Say, what's this?" asked the middle-aged manager. He sat at a metal desk piled on one side with lobby cards and on the other with requisitions, likely for candy and popcorn and soda pop.

"Question, sir," Sumida said, forcefully.

The manager straightened in his chair and narrowed his eyes. Still not satisfied with what he saw, he picked up a pair of eyeglasses from beside an open box of Milk Duds. When he got a clear look at Sumida he strained his eyes again, this time for other reasons.

"Are you a Jap?" he asked, incredulous.

Sumida didn't understand the vehemence of racial deprecations over the past few minutes. Sure, there were places Japanese immigrants and their Nisei offspring were unwelcome—for example, the LA Country Club (except as gardeners).

And plenty of others.

Most places, actually.

But he'd never felt unwelcome in a downtown movie house. He wasn't a Negro, after all. *They* seemed to be quietly unwelcome everywhere, excepting the neighborhoods around Central Avenue.

"Look, what's going on here?" Sumida asked.

"I was going to ask you the same question," the manager answered. "Are you a Chinaman or Korean?"

"My name's Sam Sumida."

The manager's eyes narrowed. "Sumida . . . What do you want?"

"I want to see the movie I paid to see."

"What?"

That's when Sumida noticed the calendar hung on the cheaply paneled wall behind the manager's desk. It was a give-away from Adohr Dairy. A bucolic farm scene featuring contented-looking cows decorated the top half, dated squares checkered the bottom. The manager had crossed off days, presumably leading to this one. But the date indicated wasn't December 6, 1941, as Sumida knew it to be.

January 22, 1942?

"What movie did you pay to see?" the manager asked.

"*The Maltese Falcon.*"

"That closed last month," the manager answered, contemptuously. "Can't you read a marquee? You no 'speak-y' English?"

Sumida said nothing.

The manager shook his head in disgust. "Look, I don't need no crazy Jap on my premises." He pushed aside a pile of papers and picked up his telephone. "I'll call the cops."

"What day is this?" Sumida asked.

The manager indicated the calendar behind him. "Look for yourself."

"Your calendar's wrong."

"You going to leave on your own or do I call them?"

"Is this all some kind of joke?" Sumida asked.

"Why would anybody joke with the likes of you?" the manager responded. "Everybody knows your kind is born without a sense of humor. That would explain why you don't like *Woman of the Year*. Tracy and Hepburn are hilarious. But you wouldn't understand. Besides, the movie don't end until after the curfew for your kind."

Curfew?

"Look, if you want a refund for your ticket I can give it to you," the manager continued.

"I didn't come here for money."

"Then what'd you bust into my office for?" The manager didn't wait for an answer but spoke into the receiver. "Operator, give me the LAPD."

Sumida knew the cops weren't going to help him get to the bottom of this.

He left the manager's office, descended the stairs, and passed through the lobby. It wasn't true that he had no sense of humor. But whatever kind of prank the movie house was playing wasn't so damn funny. He stepped outside, almost running straight into an entering patron (small boned like a boy and dressed unusually in a cloak and cowl). "Sorry," he muttered without turning back. He continued to the sidewalk. Broadway was crowded with traffic and pedestrians, as usual. But now it was raining hard. Sumida pulled his hat down over his eyes and his suit jacket tighter around his shoulders. He'd left his raincoat at home. He hadn't needed it. Forty minutes earlier, when he'd bought his ticket to see *The Maltese Falcon*, there hadn't been a cloud in the sky. And that wasn't the only difference. On the sidewalk outside the Rialto, he noted that the lighted Christmas decorations strung across the street at fifty-yard intervals when he had entered the theater were now, like the decorations in all the store windows, gone.

Not turned off.

Gone.

Excerpt from a letter dated February 17, 1942:

. . . I'm delighted and mightily impressed
that in the face of such adversity you've
not only managed to overcome your six-week
writer's block (who wasn't knocked on his
or her backside on the morning of December
7?) but that judging from your latest submission you have so effectively reworked
the synopsis and introduced not only a
more acceptable protagonist in Jimmy Park,
but also the intense patriotism that will
appeal to today's readers. And all this in
just the past couple of weeks!

Turning your book from a conventional
detective story into a spy thriller is
also clearly the right decision. And, yes,
choosing an Anglo pen name will obviously
be a necessity as well. If you'd like to
send me a few names to choose from, feel
free. In all, I am greatly impressed by
your professionalism. I think we're going
to make a great team, young man!

My most pressing suggestion, as you move
forward, is that you maintain the modern
feel of the revised first chapters while
also introducing more traditionally exotic,
"foreign" elements, such as one finds in Sax
Rohmer's Dr. Fu Manchu series (and yes,
I'm aware that Rohmer's villain is Chinese
rather than Japanese, but I think he still
serves as a good example of pure villainy—
besides, I'm sure you recall that Dr. Fu
Manchu headed a criminal organization, the
Si-Fan or Yellow Menace, that included all
Orientals, including East Indians, Burmese,

Persians, Arabs, _and_ Japanese, so draw lib-
erally from his wildly imaginative example,
even as you continue to focus on the specifically _modern_ Japanese villains infiltrating
our nation today.

On the basis of this latest submission,
we'll get your contract out to you in the
next couple of days. Sign and return to
us and then our accounting department will
draft you a new check for $350 as an advance
against royalties.

Now, how can we most effectively work
together? My thought is that we should work
closely on this book right from the start
(rather than employing the more traditional
approach of my offering suggestions and
edits _after_ you complete a first draft). I
say this for two reasons: first, you're a
young man new to this game and this _is_ professional New York publishing. Consider:
rather than my waiting the better part of a
year for you to draft your way into numerous
dead ends that will entail your having to
wipe out whole chapters or storylines (the
usual fate of beginning novelists), why
don't you send me each chapter as you finish
it so I can comment, mark it up with my
trusty blue pencil, and return it to you
for revisions. That way, any missteps you
make will be correctible before much nar-
rative damage is done (and first-time novelists, even the best, always make missteps).
The second reason I suggest this approach
is that I believe the sooner we get this
title on the market the better. After all,
a quick victory by our forces in the Pacific
will render this book far less marketable

than if we manage to get it out while war
against the Japanese persists. Naturally,
like every American, I hope for a quick
victory. But that is why I want to shep-
herd this book as efficiently as possible.
Does that make sense to you? We two can
form a kind of assembly line, wherein, for
example, you'll write chapter three while
you're waiting for my edits on chapter two,
and then you can revise chapter two and
move on to chapter four while I edit chapter
three, etc. Believe me, I rarely make such
an offer to my authors.

Let me know what you think. Of course,
it will always be YOUR book. But let's not
delay!

Congratulations, and keep up the good
work.

Sincerely,

Maxine Wakefield

Maxine Wakefield,
Associate Editor,
Metropolitan Modern Mysteries, Inc.

P.S. My best wishes to your father for a
speedy recovery from his beating at the
hands of those marauding bullies. I've
heard broken ribs can be quite painful and
one must be careful with head injuries.
And with a fine son like you, I'm sure he's
resting easy. Who knows, Takumi? In time,
royalties from a successful book could com-
pensate for any lost income from his shuttered business. Crossed fingers!

❦

Excerpt from chapter two of *The Orchid and the Secret Agent*, a novel by William Thorne
    Metropolitan Modern Mysteries, Inc., New York, N.Y., 1945

Jimmy Park got to the movie house too late.

At first, he didn't know a crime had already taken place or that the criminal had already fled. How would he? The Tracy and Hepburn movie was still playing inside.

All *seemed* to be going as planned.

At the box office, he had flashed his consultant's ID card from the FBI and proceeded straight in, stopping in the ornate, but nearly deserted, lobby. Here, the soundtrack of the movie was audible (though the actors' dialogue was muffled through the walls). He scanned for a good vantage from which to observe the audience when they exited the movie. A narrow wooden staircase led up to a door, likely the manager's office or the entrance to the projectionist's room.

"How much longer does the movie run?" he asked a teenaged usher who stood near a pretty girl working the concession stand. There were no customers about.

The usher's Adam's apple moved up and down as he looked suspiciously at Jimmy, saying nothing.

Such suspicions were not unusual these days. Jimmy Park held it against no one. Who could blame any American for being cautious? Nonetheless, it made his life more complicated. Since the shameful events of December 7, he'd found it necessary to introduce himself to almost everyone he met, no matter how casually, to reassure them he was not a Jap. "My name's Jimmy Park," he said, holding out his hand to shake.

The usher sighed in relief. "Park . . . Korean, then?" he said, taking Jimmy's proffered hand.

"That's right. Tell me, how much longer does the movie run?"

The usher looked at his watch. "About twenty minutes."

Jimmy showed the teenager his ID card from the Feds. "I need to 'make the acquaintance' of a man currently in your audience. I think it best to do so as he comes out." He turned and, with a nod of his head, indicated the wooden staircase. "That seems like the best place to get a view."

The usher nodded. "You can go up there to Mr. Pike's office and knock. He's the manager."

"Thanks."

"Funny thing," the usher added. "You're the third Oriental to make his way up there in the last hour."

"What?"

"Yeah, the first was a Jap who claimed to be confused about what movie was playing."

"What did he look like?" Jimmy pressed.

The boy opened his palms helplessly. "I don't know. Kind of like you, but not you."

"And the second man?" Jimmy asked.

"It was right after," the boy said.

"Real thin, no bigger than a boy, in a cloak that covered all but the eyes," the girl volunteered.

"Cloak?" Jimmy asked.

"I thought it was for the rain or something," the boy continued.

Jimmy didn't hesitate. He ran up the stairs and burst into the office.

That's when he knew he was too late.

Jimmy's eyes went to the movie-house manager's body on the floor. There was blood everywhere. Jimmy rushed to the victim's side, kneeling. "Mr. Pike!" he implored. But the man's head had been caved in by a blunt object. He was dead.

Was the assailant still here?

Jimmy rose to his feet, withdrawing the .45 from his raincoat pocket. He turned in a slow circle. No windows. Only the one door.

He looked behind the desk, behind a battered, velvet sofa, behind a filing cabinet.

The assailant was gone.

Jimmy rushed back to the door and called down to the teenagers.

"Did you see anyone leave this room?"

The two shook their heads no.

Jimmy turned back to the room. Weren't ninjas known for the ability to become almost invisible?

But that was mere legend.

Jimmy took a deep breath, steadying himself. There had to be a practical answer to the killer's disappearance. For example, wasn't it likely that the libidinous teenagers in the lobby had simply been too preoccupied with each another to notice the man's departure from the office?

Then Jimmy noticed what was written on the far wall.

He'd seen a lot in his line of work, but nothing like this.

The manager's murderer had sliced a tassel from the velvet sofa and, dipping the tassel into the pool of blood from the manager's bashed-in head, had used it as a calligraphy brush to write a series of Japanese characters on the wall. Being an expert in Oriental languages, Jimmy translated:

And so it begins for you, white devils.

Jimmy picked up the phone from the manager's desk. "Get me the LAPD," he said solemnly.

A few minutes later, the theater crowd emptied, passing through a quickly but efficiently assembled cordon of police at all exits. There were no Japanese among them.

THE REVISED—CHAPTER TWO

*No man ever steps in the same river twice, for it's not the
same river . . .*

—Heraclitus

Sam Sumida's night only got worse.

After leaving the Rialto he walked up Broadway to Seventh, drenched by the heavy rain, and then continued up past the Basilisk Club to the parking lot where he'd left his '37 Dodge Coupe less than an hour before. He removed the damp claim check from his pocket and handed it to an acne-scarred parking attendant, who wore a bright-yellow rain slicker and up-to-the-knee rubbers. Sam wondered how often the kid got to wear the wet-weather outfit. This was LA. Not Seattle, for God's sake.

Huddled beneath an umbrella rigged near the key-stand, the attendant glanced from the claim check to the board of keys. After a moment, he turned to Sumida.

"We don't got your car," he said, shrugging.

"What?"

He motioned for Sumida to look at the keys hanging on the numbered board.

"See, nothing there that matches this number."

"Maybe you hung the keys on the wrong peg," Sumida suggested.

"You see them hanging anywhere?"

Sumida surveyed the board. His keys were not there.

"You can look in the lot if you want to," the attendant offered.

"I don't want to look in the lot," Sumida answered. "I dropped off the car an hour ago. It's your . . ."

"Wait a minute," the attendant interrupted, looking more closely at the claim check. "This ticket is for December sixth. You can't leave a car here for that long." He handed it back to Sumida. "You'll have to come back tomorrow, when the manager's here, to figure this out."

"But you handed me that ticket just an hour ago. The date on it must be wrong."

"Me? No," the attendant said. "I just came on shift fifteen minutes ago."

"Well, somebody did."

The attendant shrugged. "Yeah, almost two months ago."

Sumida considered the calendar in the theater manager's office.

The inexplicably sudden rain storm . . .

The absence of Christmas decorations on Broadway . . .

Still, he knew what he knew. It was Saturday night, December 6, 1941. Otherwise, where did that leave him?

"Look, the keys aren't here," the attendant said impatiently, as he pointed again to the board. "And your car's not here, and your ticket is invalid as far as I'm concerned. So you're just going to have to take this up with the manager tomorrow."

A well-dressed man and woman, holding tight to one another beneath their umbrella, walked up to the stand, handing their ticket to the attendant to claim their car. The kid grabbed a set of keys off the board and started at a jog into the lot. Before he went, however, he muttered loud enough to be heard even in the rain, "Jap."

Sumida turned to the well-dressed couple, shaking his head in patient disapproval of the slur.

But the couple only looked away, disgust crossing their faces.

Sumida didn't understand what was going on tonight, in this city that he'd always thought of as his home.

He noticed a phone booth across the street.

He glanced again around the lot—no '37 Dodge.

He needed answers, or at least to hear a familiar voice.

Dashing across the street, he leaped over an oil-slicked puddle at the corner and onto the far sidewalk. Once inside the booth, at last out of the rain, he dug a dime out of his pocket and dialed the number of his friend Tony Fortuna, who lived with his wife and two kids across the street from Sumida in Echo Park. Sometimes, Tony went with Sumida to LA Angels baseball games at Wrigley Field over on Avalon and Forty-First. They both agreed that "Peanuts" Lowrey wasn't going to be in the Pacific Coast League for long but was bound for the Majors.

The coin clattered into the phone.

Tony picked up on the second ring. "'Lo?"

"Tony, it's me, Sam."

"Who?"

"*Sam*," he snapped, impatiently. "Listen, buddy, I need a ride. It's been a tough night. Are you free to . . ."

"Sam *who*?" Tony interrupted.

"Sumida," he answered.

There was silence on the other end.

"Tony?" Sumida pressed.

"I don't know no Sam Sumida," his friend said.

"Of course you do, from across the street. The ball games . . ."

"Sumida . . . that's a Jap name?"

"Look Tony, it's *me*. What's wrong with you?"

"What's wrong with you!" Tony shouted. "I don't know no Japs," he snarled before hanging up.

Sumida dug out another dime and called back.

"What!" Tony snapped as he answered.

"Look Tony, don't hang up. I need help."

Tony laughed. "If you're a Jap in this town these days, I think you're right."

"So, please . . ."

"But I ain't lying," Tony interrupted. "You got the wrong number."

"Wait, what's today's date, Tony?" Sumida asked.

"What is this, some kind of prank? It's January twenty-second," Tony said, before hanging up again.

Sumida put the receiver back on the cradle. But he didn't leave the booth. He took a long, deep breath. Things outside of this booth were cockeyed, as if he'd fallen down a rabbit hole and discovered himself in a dark, Wonderland-version of his life. He could call somebody else. He had former colleagues from local colleges. But he didn't know how to explain what was happening without sounding mad as a hatter.

The best thing to do was to go home, get some sleep, and wake tomorrow in a world that made sense.

Pulling his drenched jacket tighter around his shoulders, he stepped out of the phone booth, bending into the wind-blown rain and pushing the brim of his hat down so far that he could see only two steps ahead on the sidewalk. His bungalow in Echo Park was at least four miles away, so he made for the number 7 streetcar. The offices and stores were closed, but there were plenty of bars and people around. When the streetcar arrived, it was crowded.

He stepped through the door and onto the top step, reaching into his pocket for a coin.

"Hey, there's no room," said a young man standing near the entrance in a neatly pressed Army uniform, his girl hanging on his arm. "Can't you see this streetcar is for Americans only?"

"I am an American," Sumida said, wearying of this nightmare.

"You a Chink?" the soldier asked. "I can never tell the difference."

"My name's Sam Sumida."

"Get off before I *throw* you off," the soldier snapped, his girlfriend grinning and pressing closer into his broad shoulder. "You don't belong out at this hour anyway. It'd be within my rights to shoot you dead."

Sumida glanced deeper into the streetcar.

Even the Negroes on board looked at him as if he had crossed some line.

"Look . . ." Sumida started.

He was interrupted by the streetcar operator, who pushed him in the chest and off the bottom step of the streetcar.

"I don't want no trouble," the operator said, looking at his watch. "Don't you know the time? It's five minutes to eight."

Sumida looked at his watch. "What happens at eight?"

"Curfew for Japs, dumb shit," the operator said.

This curfew business mentioned again . . . He wanted to ask what it was all about. But he didn't think he'd like the answer he got from this crowd, which would likely be no answer at all.

The streetcar started away without Sumida. He watched it go.

So he'd walk. Already drenched, he couldn't get any wetter. Maybe a cab would happen by . . .

It was after eleven when he finally walked up McDuff Street. He noticed that his house was all alight inside.

He didn't remember having turned on any lights before he left.

❧

Excerpt from chapter three of *The Orchid and the Secret Agent*, a novel by William Thorne

  Metropolitan Modern Mysteries, Inc., New York, N.Y., 1945

. . . Jimmy considered: The manager had likely been murdered only to inform the Feds that the assassin knew they were after him. Immediately, Jimmy thought of the welfare of his informant.

He rushed down the wooden stairs to the Rialto lobby.

All to no avail.

Within the hour, LAPD found the body of Jimmy's "eyes and ears," José "Gypsy" Martinez, a skid-row regular who frequented the backstreets of nearby Little Tokyo, Jap Town. The corpse had been stuffed in six pieces (head, four limbs, and torso) into an orange crate in an alley off Seventh. The first officers on the scene, upon examining the body parts, indicated the weapon had likely been a long, sharp blade.

Samurai sword, Jimmy thought. *Poor Gypsy*.

Written on the alley wall in the victim's blood, in the same steady hand, was another message, which translated

We are watching your eyes, even as they fail to see us.

Excerpt from a letter dated March 31, 1942:

. . . a good list, though I have to disagree
on your proposed final choice. While I think
Richard Barratt is a perfectly good name
for a <u>character</u>, it's a little weak as a pen
name. Sure, its respectability and Anglo-
Saxon pedigree are impeccable. Perhaps you
can give it to a high-level agent . . . But
I believe your discarded choice, William
Thorne, is actually much stronger for use
as a pseudonym. Over my years in the business, I've noted that readers find characters who have long vowel sounds in their
names to be stronger, and the long "o" in
"Thorne" works just that way. Additionally,
that "thorn" is a word makes the name easier
for readers to remember. And <u>that</u> is important, as I can imagine this book spawning
a whole series featuring Jimmy Park vs.
evildoers.

As for your proposed changes to your new
outline, which would condense all the action
into a single, twenty-four-hour period, I'm
quite enthused! I wish I'd thought of it
myself. (What kind of sorry editor am I,
anyway?) But seriously, for a first-time
novelist like yourself, that kind of tight
time chronology will surely serve to discipline your focus on continually moving the
<u>story</u> forward. And that's what bestsellers
are made of!!!

Sincerely,

Maxine Wakefield
Maxine Wakefield,
Associate Editor,
Metropolitan Modern Mysteries, Inc.

P.S. I did not miss your fanciful questions regarding what I think becomes of
characters who've been cut from never-
to-be-written drafts (i.e. Sumida and the
murderous Czernicek). I <u>do</u> agree that a
well-drawn character achieves a kind of
life that is ultimately independent of his
author. You're right about Huck Finn being
"alive" today in a way that Twain is not.
Is that merely because the famous novel is
still read? Or, instead, might the ani-
mating force be the result of the character's creation alone or even his author's
initial conception of the character,
regardless of ultimate readership? And, if
that is so, then where <u>are</u> these characters that an author conceives, only later
to cut? Good questions. I don't know. Nor
can we ever know. Maybe such characters
don't go anywhere, but remain where they've
always been, relegated to unwitting background roles. Or maybe they just molder on
a wadded sheet of typing paper in a trash
can, soon incinerated with the rest of the
garbage.

THE REVISED—CHAPTER TWO cont'd.

The rain had stopped and Sam Sumida stood for a moment on the sidewalk outside his house. Aside from the lights burning inside, everything looked as he had left it. He couldn't help thinking about Kyoko, who had picked out the bungalow from among those in Echo Park they could afford. The neighborhood was reasonably safe and centrally located, with a lovely urban park near enough that he and his wife planned to one day walk there hand-in-hand with their children. But there were no children and there never would be. There was no Kyoko.

Still, Sam couldn't help remembering.

They had held a housewarming party in the backyard just three years before. Friends and family had come. Dr. Shinoda, whose thriving Little Tokyo dental practice Kyoko managed, brought champagne and toothbrushes for everyone. The head of the art department at UCLA had brought, as a housewarming present, a print signed by Diego Rivera. It hung in the living room. Kyoko loved the print. She loved the house. She loved Sam too, at least for a while. But some bastard with a .22 ended all possibilities of their ever being happy again. Why? It had fallen to Sam to find out.

He took a deep breath.

This night had been confusing, disheartening, soaking wet. But it was just one night. His mind was playing tricks. A good sleep would change everything. He reminded himself that he had no pressing problems save one: finding Kyoko's killer. Nothing else mattered.

He started forward, then stopped.

Somehow, the house didn't feel the same.

Of course, the place had become something different eleven months before. His aunt and uncle had suggested he sell, that sleeping in the room he had shared with Kyoko couldn't be healthy. *Sugitaru wa nao oyobazaru ga gotoshi.* "Let what is past flow away downstream," his aunt said, being aggravatingly fond of maxims. But he didn't *want* to let go, to move forward. The only movement he wanted was backward, and that was impossible. So he hadn't sold the place, even when his aunt further pressed him, reminding him of Kyoko's unfaithful-ness: *Akusai wa hyaku-non no fusaku*. "A bad wife spells a hundred years of bad harvest." But Sam didn't see Kyoko that way, whatever turn their marriage had taken. He stayed in the house. Nonetheless, it had recently begun to feel like "his" instead of "theirs"—perhaps an inevi-table consequence of time.

Now, irrationally, it didn't even feel like his anymore either.

Regaining his sense of the present, he noticed a 1939 Chrysler Royal parked in the driveway.

Whose car?

At the front door, he reached into his pocket for his keys. But he'd left them with the parking attendant downtown at *some* point in the past. So he knelt and reached beside the garden hose for the rock beneath which hid his spare house key. Nothing there. "Shit," he muttered.

He tried the door.

Fortunately, and unexpectedly, it was unlocked.

When he walked into his house, the first thing he noticed was a tall, white man in slacks, blue dress shirt, and suspenders, lying sprawled face up, snoring, on the sofa, an empty bottle of rye on the floor beside him.

"Hey, what are you doing in my house?" Sumida asked, kicking at the white man sleeping on the sofa.

The big man didn't budge, but merely snored more loudly.

Sumida turned.

That's when he noticed that the Diego Rivera print had been replaced on the wall by a quartet of framed, hand-embroidered sam-plers, all bearing clichéd sayings like, "Home Sweet Home" and "God Bless America." Who'd moved the picture? Then he noticed some-thing even more disturbing. Where were his wedding photos? And, on the mantelpiece, where were the half-dozen antique Japanese wood and ivory carvings, *netsuke*, which had been Kyoko's sole inheritance when her parents were killed in an automobile accident? The furniture and curtains were different too, ugly and obviously chosen without a woman's eye, without Kyoko's eye. Propped informally against the radio was a snapshot of an unfamiliar, romantically entwined Asian couple. He picked it up. In ink, the woman had inscribed, "To Jimmy, with much love, Sun." Who? Cigar butts crowded ash trays. When had Sumida's home become a bachelor pad? It made no sense.

Sam moved through the house.

To his shock and dismay, he found no sign of his living here—nor of Kyoko. But there was plenty of evidence of some other man. In a framed photograph on the dresser in the master bedroom stood an unfamiliar Asian man dressed in a t-shirt and chino pants in front of *this* house, Sam's house, removing a "For Sale" sign with a wide grin on his face and a '37 Dodge Coupe in the background.

That's when he heard the toilet flush in the bathroom.

He turned.

The door opened and Tony Fortuna emerged, his face red from drinking.

"Tony!" Sam said, pleased to see his friend's familiar mug.

Tony narrowed his eyes. "Who are you?"

"It's me, Sam."

"Who? I don't know no Sam."

"Come on, Tony. It's *me*, Sam Sumida."

"You called me a couple hours back?"

"I can see you've been drinking, Tony."

Tony shrugged. "Maybe I've had a few, but not so many as to be confused about Japs." Showing surprising dexterity for a drunk, he slipped past Sam and into the living room. "Hey, Joe, wake up!" he called.

Sam followed him.

Tony knelt beside the big man and was now shaking him by the lapels. "Wake *up*!"

The man on the couch opened his eyes momentarily. His pupils were rolled halfway back into his head.

"Look, what's going on?" Sam pressed. "Who's this big guy? In *my* house."

Tony turned. "*Your* house?"

Sam nodded.

"Look, what do you want, Sumida?" Tony asked, as if addressing a threatening stranger. "Did you come here looking for Jimmy? Or is he looking for you? I know he's been doing some kind of 'special' work. Whose side are you on?"

"Who's Jimmy?"

Tony fumbled inside the unconscious man's jacket, his jittery hand emerging with a .38 Special, which he turned on Sumida.

"Look, Tony . . ."

"Shut up." Tony stood. "If I pull this trigger it'll blow your brains clean out the back of your head. So put your hands up."

Sumida raised his hands. "You've been drinking, Tony. So maybe you don't recognize me."

"I'm not as drunk as all that. Now, sit down in that chair and keep your hands where I can see them."

Hadn't Sam just seen Humphrey Bogart knock the gun from the hand of Peter Lorre? But Tony was too far to reach. Besides, real life felt different than movies, even if Tony swayed where he stood, more drunk than he was willing to admit.

"I said, *sit*," Tony repeated, as if talking to a dog.

Had there been some object Sumida could grab he'd have hurled it at him and then taken away the gun. But there was nothing within reach. So he'd have to bide his time, wait for his moment. Good PIs did that too, sometimes.

He sat.

Tony took a deep breath, uncertain what to do next, and then belched.

"This is my home," Sumida said, confused. "But someone's changed everything. Who let you in?"

"I'll ask the questions," Tony snapped.

Then the moment Sam had been awaiting arrived.

The phone rang.

Tony turned.

Sumida leaped toward him, acting on instincts developed in his

youth at a karate dojo in the Bixby Knolls section of Long Beach. He
didn't know that Tony wouldn't just turn and shoot him dead. But he
didn't consider outcomes. He just acted.

He kicked the gun from Tony's hand.

With the handgun now on the floor across the room, roughly
equidistant between the two men, Tony took an old-fashioned boxing
stance, like John L. Sullivan. He snarled and motioned for his Japanese opponent to approach. Sumida obliged, moving in, his hands and
feet flashing in coordinated arcs that leveled his opponent. A final kick
to the sinking man rendered him unconscious. He fell hard, his head
cracking audibly against the stone fireplace hearth.

The telephone stopped ringing.

Sam didn't understand what was happening. But he knew this
wasn't his house. Not anymore. Just as Tony was no longer his friend,
or even acquaintance, apparently.

Sumida knew he needed help.

Picking up the telephone, he dialed the number of his aunt and
uncle, who cared for his ailing mother and had been like another set of
parents to him.

But the phone didn't even ring. Instead, an operator informed him
that no such number was in service.

"That's impossible," he said, hanging up.

He dialed again, making certain he got it right this time.

Different operator, same message . . .

He'd drive to his aunt and uncle's house in South Gate, fifteen
miles away. He had to see someone who recognized him.

He knelt and took the car keys from the pocket of the man still
unconscious on the couch.

Next, he picked up the handgun that had skittered across the living
room floor.

Outside, he started the big man's '39 Chrysler. As he backed out
of the driveway, he noticed in the rearview mirror a shadowed figure
standing across the street; the figure was further obscured by what
appeared to be a hooded rain cloak. Small and lean, almost feline. He·

was reminded of the entering movie-house patron with whom he'd collided on his way out of the lobby. It couldn't be the same person. In any case, it was a witness . . . But he didn't stop, as he hadn't an explanation for any of it. So he gunned the car down the street. At a traffic light a few miles east on Temple, he checked the car's registration on the steering column. The owner was named Joe Lucas.

Inside the glove compartment was a leather ID wallet that contained a badge.

Lucas was LAPD.

"Shit," Sumida murmured.

Excerpt from chapter four of *The Orchid and the Secret Agent*, a novel by William Thorne

Metropolitan Modern Mysteries, Inc., New York, N.Y., 1945

The first thing Jimmy Park noticed as he pulled up to his house was that Joe's car was no longer parked in the driveway and that all the lights were on inside. He sighed. When drunk, his friend couldn't be trusted with even the simplest things. He doubted Joe had locked up after himself. But at least Joe had managed to leave the house. Once a week, Joe passed out on the sofa, awakening with hangovers that would have killed a lesser man. Jimmy wondered how Joe's wife put up with it. He could barely tolerate it himself.

But, friendship was friendship.

And, after what Jimmy had seen in the past few hours in the manager's office at the movie theatre and then in the bloody alley off Seventh Street, he thought it might not have been the worst thing in the world to have had a buddy in the house tonight. Even a rye-soaked, unconscious one, which was, despite the absent Chrysler Royal, precisely what he found when he walked in the front door.

Joe sprawled, snoring, on his belly on the sofa, one arm hanging over the edge, his hand resting like a porcelain sculpture on the carpet beside the empty bottle. But that wasn't what Jimmy focused on when he first walked into the room. Nor did he wonder where Joe's car was.

That was child's play.

This was not . . .

Written in blood on the wall behind the sofa, a mere three feet over Joe's head, were more Japanese characters. The calligraphy was the same as at the movie house. Translated, it read, "Accept your friend's life as a personal gift."

"Joe!" Jimmy called. "Wake up."

Joe kept on snoring.

Jimmy removed the .45 from the pocket of his raincoat and turned in a slow circle in the room.

The assassin could still be here.

Cautiously, Jimmy inspected the living room, kitchenette, dining room, master bedroom, bathroom, guest bedroom. He went to the back door and ran the flashlight over the backyard. Aside from an opossum scurrying away from the light, he spied nothing unusual.

Still, his senses remained sharp.

There were shadows everywhere.

He went back inside, locking the back door behind him, and returned to the living room, shaking his friend by the shoulder and emphatically calling his name, "Joe, Joe, Joe."

At last the big man opened his eyes, though he didn't seem capable of moving another muscle. "Jimmy?"

"Yeah, what happened here, Joe?"

Joe managed to brush the empty bottle of rye with his hand, rolling it toward Jimmy. "The usual, I guess. Sorry."

That wasn't what Jimmy was asking. But it was evidence enough that Joe wasn't aware *anything* unusual had happened. He'd slept through it. He'd be no help.

Jimmy glanced up to the blood-scrawled message on the wall.

Joe closed his eyes again, snoring.

How easy it would have been for the assassin to cut his friend's throat.

But this *personal gift* business . . .

Jimmy owed the Jap assassin nothing but a bullet between the eyes. That would be *his* personal gift.

Then he noticed something unusual about the calligraphy.

He hadn't caught the subtlety of style back at the movie house or in the alley, though he knew the writing was the same. Perhaps he'd been too distracted by the waves of police and technicians who descended upon the places. Or maybe he just needed to see the calligraphy a third time to realize it had been written by a woman.

He couldn't say for sure how he knew.

But he was certain.

He recalled that the teenagers who worked in the movie-house lobby described the "man" who went into the manager's office as being thin and wearing a cloak.

They hadn't seen his face. Or *her* face.

And then Jimmy had a terrible thought.

The assassin had used the blood of his victims to write the messages back at the movie house and in the alley.

Where had *this* blood come from?

Jimmy didn't have to look long to discover the answer.

A puddle was forming at the edges of the sofa.

"Joe!" he called again, rolling his friend onto the ground and kneeling to run his hands over his body, frantically looking for a wound.

Joe opened one eye. "Hey, you trying to take advantage of me, buddy?" he kidded, unaware of all that was going on. "You think I'm some kind of cheap date or something?"

Ignoring Joe's joking, Jimmy sighed in relief when he found no wounds.

But then he noticed the sofa.

After Joe had rolled off it, the cushions rose up a few inches, as if something had been stuffed inside, held down until now by Joe's dead weight.

Jimmy got to his feet and removed one cushion, which was enough.

Stuffed inside the sofa was his neighbor from across the street, Tony Fortuna, who sometimes came over with a bottle of amaretto when he noticed Joe's big car parked outside. The two liked to talk about Minor League baseball.

Tony's throat had been cut.

It was his blood on the walls. Used by a female hand for a perfect and terrible message in calligraphy.

This spy ring Jimmy had been alerted to . . .

They were onto him. They meant business.

He was glad his girlfriend Sun wasn't over tonight. What horrors might they have done to her?

Locking the side and then front doors, he went for the phone.

❧

Excerpt from a letter dated April 12, 1942:

> . . . I am saddened to hear that you and your parents will be forced to leave your home in the next few days. Naturally, you were the first person I thought of when I heard about the President's executive order on the radio. Somehow, I didn't anticipate the relocations taking place so quickly. I understand too that you're disappointed at having to discontinue your art history studies at UCLA. (Though, frankly, this may be a blessing in disguise, as your natural instincts as a novelist are such that I do not believe art history is the right field for you or, for that matter, that a college education is necessary to your success as a writer—look at Hemingway, no college at all! Academia can be a trap, dear boy.) Now, you will have all the time that your writing requires.
>
> Still, these <u>are</u> difficult times (so sad that you have to leave your dog behind), and your resilience will likely be further tested. But try to remain positive. Perhaps

getting away from familiar places (some of
them clearly dangerous these days, a case
in point being your father's violent experience with the marauding anti-Japanese
bullies in LA, whom I read in TIME Magazine are becoming only more prevalent) will
stimulate your work rather than restrict it.
After all, I have, to date, been impressed
by the versatility of your vision and feel
confident that in no time you'll be re-set-
tled and back to the daily rhythms that
have produced such excellent first chapters.

Bear up, Takumi Sato, and keep up the
good work. Ah to have the energy of a twenty-
two year-old and talent! I believe you can
really make something of this novel.

Sincerely,

Maxine Wakefield
Maxine Wakefield,
Associate Editor,
Metropolitan Modern Mysteries, Inc.

THE REVISED—CHAPTER THREE

And if, through the act of a powerful magician or perverse,
authorial god, your world came to belong to another man,
rendering you unrecognizable even to friends and family,
would you still bear the strength to be . . . you?
　　　　　　　　　　　　　　　　—James Matsumoto, chaplain at
　　　　　　　　　　　　　　　　Manzanar Relocation Camp

Leaving Echo Park, Sam Sumida drove south for ten or twelve miles, past dark, open lots and auto repair shops and junkyards that were shuttered for the night, likely guarded by heavily muscled dogs. Very few cars passed in either direction. Turning onto Florence, the businesses tended now more toward retail stores, radio repair shops, and a few gasoline stations that were open even at this hour. Occasional lights still glowed in houses interspersed among the local businesses.

It was just past midnight when Sam Sumida shut off the Chrysler in South Gate.

Of course, it was far too late for an ordinary visit, but this was no time to stand on ceremony.

Uncle Yamato and Aunt Misaki had taken in Sumida's ailing mother, Sakura, a few months earlier, when it became clear that the poor woman's mental state would no longer allow her to live on her own. Sam would have taken her in himself had it not been for the pressing matter of finding his wife's killer, which took all of his time. He was grateful his mother and her younger sister Misaki had always been so close. And Uncle Yamato was a generous man who had been like a second father to Sam, particularly after Sam's actual father had been killed in an accident at sea.

Sumida's family was small but close.

He got out of the unfamiliar car and made his way to the neatly kept, Spanish-style bungalow. He pressed the doorbell.

After a moment, a middle-aged Asian man, unfamiliar to Sumida, opened the door. He wore a dressing gown, and his hair was disheveled. He frowned at Sam. "What do you want?" he asked, holding firm to the door. "Do you know what time it is?"

"Who are you?" Sumida inquired, surprised.

"I said, 'What do you want?'" the man repeated.

"I've come here to see my Uncle Yamato," Sumida said cautiously.

"Who?"

"This is his home," Sumida said, starting forward. "What are you doing here?"

But the stranger stopped him with an extended hand.

"Surely you know my Aunt Misaki," Sam continued.

"We are Korean-Americans in this household, not Japs. I'm unfamiliar with the names you cite."

"But my mother lives here too."

"Are you mad? We've been here for six years and we've never shared our home with Japs," the stranger said, slamming the door shut.

Sumida stood for a long time on the porch, not knowing what else to do. He saw the curtains at the front window stir. He was being watched. Who were these people? Likely they'd call the police if he didn't leave. So he returned to the stolen car. This was not the place to demand an explanation.

He drove back to Echo Park, *his* home.

He turned right off of Belleview Avenue onto Laveta Terrace—his street.

But as he rounded the corner, he saw the flashing red lights of three police squad cars in front of his bungalow, one parked in his driveway and the other two angled on his carefully tended front lawn.

He pulled over to the curb, six or seven houses down from his own, and shut off his lights and engine.

Neighbors in dressing gowns and robes stood on their front porches or gathered in small groups on the sidewalk, chattering, speculating.

Sumida settled low in his seat, watching.

A half-dozen motorcycle cops muscled wooden barricades to block off his property. After a moment, an ambulance turned the corner at the far end of the street, cruising slowly up to the curb space in front of the house. No urgency. No life to save. Instead, they calmly removed a gurney from the back of the vehicle and rolled it into the house.

Had Tony Fortuna's fall against the fireplace killed him?

Fall wasn't the right word. No, it had been Sumida's blow that had sent Tony sprawling.

He put his head in his hands.

After a few minutes, the ambulance attendants emerged from the house with the gurney. Loaded atop it was a body, covered head to foot by a white sheet that was stained red in its upper third.

The Asian man, who had been in the framed photo where once Sam's wedding picture had stood, emerged now with a uniformed officer and a short, barrel-chested man in a business suit, who displayed his detective's badge on his suit coat pocket.

They watched the gurney being loaded onto the ambulance.

Sumida started the stolen car without turning on the lights. He backed away along the curb and then cut backward into a neighbor's driveway, from which he pulled forward and down the street in the direction from which he'd come. He kept his eyes in the rearview mirror, expecting any minute to see flashing red lights trailing him. But no one followed.

❧

Excerpt from chapter five of *The Orchid and the Secret Agent*, a novel by William Thorne
Metropolitan Modern Mysteries, Inc., New York, N.Y., 1945

Jimmy Park had been summoned more than once to police headquarters, the local FBI office, or the Department of War office to meet with high-level officials about difficult cases or even national threats. His talent for languages, unusual appearance, and knowledge of Oriental cultures (enabling him to infiltrate Chinese Tong or Japanese Yakuza operations) sometimes made him indispensable. However, he had never received a summons like the one he got the morning after the murder of his neighbor Tony, whose body had been stuffed so unceremoniously into the sofa.

Naturally, the LAPD had been first on the scene and so first to question Jimmy. Three blood-thirsty murders in one night. . . . Jimmy had many friends on the force, so the questioning went smoothly. (Naturally, he couldn't tell the police all he knew about the spy ring, as that was classified.) He also left out the part about Joe literally sleeping, drunk, atop the body. Joe himself didn't know that part, as Jimmy had dragged him into the bedroom to save him embarrassment before the police arrived. Joe was a proud man and Jimmy knew that to have been reported in such an embarrassing position would have broken his spirit, a true loss to the force.

Early the following morning, the FBI sent agents to question Jimmy; they focused more on the message written in blood, but otherwise asked many of the same questions that the LAPD had asked. Finally, Jimmy expected the Department of War to call, specifically Colonel Holloway, with whom he'd been working clandestinely these past weeks on the Japanese spy ring.

But that wasn't what happened.

Mere moments after the FBI agents left, a big, black Cadillac pulled into Jimmy's driveway. Jimmy had expected a US Army vehicle. He watched from his front window as two dark-suited men, wearing felt fedoras pulled so low that their eyes were barely visible, emerged from the car and knocked at Jimmy's door.

Jimmy answered, his .45 tucked into his waistband at the small of his back.

The men both looked like they'd played on the offensive line for Yale.

"Mr. Park, we'd like you to come with us," one said.

Meanwhile, the other removed a business card:

Richard Barratt
United States Secret Service, Special Operations

"Need I bring anything?" Jimmy asked.

The agent shook his head. "You may bring the .45 you have tucked into the back of your pants, if it makes you feel better."

Hmmm, Jimmy thought. *These guys are good.*

"Otherwise," the agent continued, "You need only bring your love of country."

"That, gentlemen, I bring with me everywhere," Jimmy answered, glancing back at the Japanese characters painted on his wall before stepping outside, double locking the door behind him, and starting with the two agents toward the big, black car. "Where, exactly, are we going, Agent Barratt?"

"Oh, I'm not Barratt," the agent answered, grinning. "He's the boss, and you'll be meeting him shortly."

"Then what's your name?" Jimmy asked.

"Not important," the agent said, opening the back door of the car and indicating for Jimmy to get in.

The other agent went around to the driver's side.

"What now, you going to blindfold me?" Jimmy asked, kiddingly.

"As a matter of fact, yes," the agent whose name was not Barratt answered, removing a blindfold from his inside jacket pocket. "For your own protection."

"Say, what kind of special ops is this?" Jimmy inquired.

❧

Excerpt from a letter June 23, 1942:

> . . . and on another note, I'm delighted
> to report that at last week's editorial
> meeting, the publisher asked about our
> project and inquired as to who this William

Thorne, the author, is. I didn't tell him
that Thorne is a nom de plume for you, dear
boy, but reported that the name is a pseudonym for an actual police detective in the
LAPD currently assigned to the anti-espio-
nage unit of the force. The idea came to me
in a blaze of inspiration. Everyone at the
table loved it. (One or two among my colleagues know the truth, but I've convinced
them to remain mum on Thorne's "backstory,"
even if doing so pushes the boundaries of
what's commonly considered "respectable
publishing.") So, in a sense, I think there
is another character for you to create. Who
is William Thorne? When it comes time to
promote the book, perhaps we can use the
"biographical" material to our advantage,
particularly as Thorne's supposed expertise will add credence to the authenticity
of the Japanese threat in our homeland.
He should be a real hard-boiled type. So
start thinking about this Thorne fellow,
your shadow persona. Have fun with it. And
send me a brief draft of his author bio,
which we'll have plenty of time to play
with before the pub date. (In other words,
don't let it distract you from your most
important work at hand, The Orchid and the
Secret Agent!)

Sincerely,

Maxine Wakefield
Maxine Wakefield,
Associate Editor,
Metropolitan Modern Mysteries, Inc.

☙

THE REVISED—CHAPTER THREE cont'd.

Sumida managed to fall asleep in the backseat of the car.

He'd driven to a truck stop thirty minutes northeast of downtown, parking between tractor-trailers where he was less likely to be spotted by cops on the lookout for a stolen '39 Chrysler Royal. He could have driven to the house of an associate from one or another of the colleges where he'd taught, but he wouldn't know how to explain why he was calling so late, or even what was happening to him. How, for example, his house had ceased to be *his* house. Or how it had become January when the last thing he remembered was early December. It was late, and he was exhausted from the long, soaked walk from the movie house on Broadway to his home in Echo Park and then by the shock and physical confrontation that had awaited him there, the additional disorientation at what *had* been the home of his aunt and uncle in South Gate, and, finally, by the possibility that he had inadvertently killed his delirious friend Tony Fortuna. The night had started like any other. How had it become like this? So he'd decided the best course of action was the one he yearned for most: sleep. Perhaps by closing his eyes he'd accomplish more than just rest. Perhaps sleep would set things right and he'd awaken, either in his own car or, better still, in his own bed, and the mysterious discrepancies of the past hours would be wiped away by the light of an ordinary morning.

He dreamed of his wife, Kyoko.

In the dream, they walked together, hand-in-hand, on the rutted dirt road that cut through her father's strawberry field in Garden Grove. She was talking about a bluebird nest she'd found in a tree near her bedroom window. He was so happy to be with her. In the dream, he told her that the nest reminded him of how they'd met in Long Beach at the Bluebird Café. (Actually, they'd met at White's Point Resort in

San Pedro, at a chaste summer dance party for Nisei students from junior high schools all over southern California, but such are dreams that actual histories don't much matter.) Continuing hand-in-hand across the strawberry field, he confessed to her that he didn't know his way back to the place from which they'd commenced their walk (wide-open and easily navigable as strawberry fields *actually* are), and she had answered with one of her stoic mother's favorite sayings: *shikata ga nai*, this cannot be helped.

Shikata ga nai, he thought, awakening.

Opening his eyes, he noted that the sun had not yet risen. And, worse, he was still in the backseat of the '39 Chrysler Royal, dressed in the still-damp clothes he'd worn to the movie house the night before. Nonetheless, he clambered from the backseat over to the front seat.

He needed to understand more before he moved about in daylight.

So he slipped the key into the ignition, turning it half-way to engage the battery without starting the engine, and, still prone and out of sight on the bench seat, he reached to the dashboard and switched on the radio. He knew that even a faint glow posed a risk of giving away his presence. But he needed to hear a human voice. Besides, there'd be little movement among the truckers until sunrise. He planned to pull away before then. After a few seconds, the radio warmed up and he turned the dial to KFI, where he found the news.

An announcer said it was Friday, January 23, 1942.

"Rise and shine, Los Angeles," my ass, Sumida thought.

It *should* have been Sunday morning, December 7, 1941. It *should* have been a peaceful, quiet morning spent with the *LA Times* and a glass of juice squeezed from oranges grown on a tree in the backyard of his own house. But whatever nightmare had commenced the night before continued.

And then it got worse.

The newsman said something about a war in the Pacific.

Sumida sat up on the front seat, listening:

Thousands of civilians had been killed in Singapore by merciless Japanese bombings.

American forces had engaged Japanese combatants in the Bataan Peninsula.

American forces against Japanese?

The radio news continued:

Unconfirmed reports suggested that Japanese forces had massacred *thousands* at Changjiao in China.

Locally, two sports fishermen reported a Japanese submarine off the coast of Santa Barbara.

And, at a press conference yesterday, LA's chief of police warned that with the increasing possibility of an imminent Japanese military invasion of the mainland, vigilant residents of Southern California needed to report not only unusual activities sighted along the coastline but *any* suspicious behavior among their Japanese-American neighbors, even those of long standing. The chief revealed that Army Intelligence warned there was little doubt that some percentage of local Japanese-American farmers, fishermen, small business owners, and service workers were, in fact, deceitful Fifth Columnists.

The racial epithets from the night before made sense. American-born or not, Sumida was now the enemy.

Finally, the newsman reported that sometime after ten p.m. a local man had died of a skull fracture sustained in a fall at the home of a neighbor on the eight hundred block of Laveta Terrace in the Echo Park neighborhood. Currently, police were not treating the death as a homicide, but as a likely "domestic accident." Unconfirmed reports suggested alcohol was likely a factor. Authorities had not yet released the name of the unfortunate Angeleno.

Sumida knew the name—Tony Fortuna.

And while there had been drinking, he also knew it was not alcohol that had cracked Tony's skull.

He gathered himself.

Sumida's country was at war and he'd inadvertently killed his neighbor (who somehow hadn't recognized him). Sumida needed to do something. Ought he to turn himself in? But what would that accomplish? Particularly as he no longer understood *how the world worked*.

What had become of the last six weeks?

How had so much changed?

He'd heard of blackouts—periods when individuals seemed to "lose time," learning upon reawakening that they'd moved unconsciously about their worlds in uncharacteristic ways. The Jekyll and Hyde business, which might explain the lost time (a period of evident catastrophe in world affairs) but little else of his interactions with the seemingly altered world. No, his dislocation extended beyond a mere temporary blackout. But what did that leave?

Perhaps he'd have been better off not waking at all, either from his night's brief sleep or the two-month blackout that preceded it. But he *had* awakened. And his instinct for survival, for which he'd carried shame since the murder of his wife, remained too.

So now he considered immediate precautions.

With dawn just minutes away, he slipped out of the car, closing the door softly behind him to shut off the dome light. He looked around to insure no one could see him. Wedged between the tractor-trailers, he couldn't see far. He looked straight up. Judging from the visible stars, the new day would be mercifully absent of rain. But mud was still everywhere. He bent and grabbed a handful, moving around to the back of the car and crouching to the level of the California license place, which read:

"82B3874."

Applying the mud carefully, like a painter working in unusual materials, he managed to change the yellow letters on the black plate, until it read:

"32P3371"

He'd seen the trick in one or another movie. Or he'd read it in a book. He didn't remember. And though he knew it wouldn't fool the cops for long, it'd buy him a little time on the roads without his Chrysler being spotted as a stolen vehicle (so long as the mud dried dark enough and held fast). Later, he'd have to stop at a five-and-dime and buy a small can of black paint. For now, he made his way to the front bumper and repeated the mud application to the front license plate.

Cautiously, he walked around the back of one tractor-trailer to get a wider view.

The first glow of morning was visible over the mountains in the east. The subtle colors and shadings of gold reminded him of the Edo-period paintings of Kanō Sanraku—more than three hundred years and a world away . . . a useless thought now.

The diner across the lot was open, and a few truck drivers had already settled at the counter inside. Sumida would not be joining them. Instead, he returned to his car, turned the key, and pulled out of the lot.

The streets were quiet, lampposts still aglow.

He drove cautiously. The last thing he could afford would be to get pulled over for a speeding ticket.

There was only one place to go now. The Evergreen Cemetery in Boyle Heights. He needed to talk to Kyoko.

Of course, she wouldn't talk back to him. He knew that much, even in this fragmented frame of mind. But at least he could put his hand on her name, where it was carved in stone—where it said, "BELOVED WIFE" (even if, during those last months, she had not actually loved him so much but had been deceived and seduced by some unknown, dishonorable, and possibly murderous suitor).

Boyle Heights lay a few miles east of downtown. The Evergreen Cemetery, largest and oldest in LA, did not open its gates until seven, so Sumida parked near a closed taco stand to wait the last few minutes. He watched the neighborhood awaken. Mexicans and whites made their ways out of their wooden frame houses, heading toward one or another of the streetcar or bus lines that would take them to work in the foundries of Gardena or the houses of the wealthy in Beverly Hills. At seven, a man in a dark suit with aviator sunglasses unlocked and opened the metal gates to the cemetery.

Sumida waited for the man to disappear inside the cemetery

before driving straight to the spot he had frequented so often these past months . . .

But there, after getting out of his car, Sumida's heart sank.

In the place on the marble wall where Kyoko's marker belonged there now hung a different marker, "Miko Kamikubo, 1901–1939."

He'd never heard of Miko Kamikubo.

And he hadn't made a mistake in searching out Kyoko's marker. He'd been here a hundred times since her passing. His heart pounded so hard that for a moment he could hardly breathe. Where was Kyoko? He ran down one long row of marble memorials and then another and another.

Why would they have moved her resting place?

Finally, he'd covered the whole Japanese section. She was gone.

He got back in the big Chrysler and drove to the cemetery office, which didn't open until 9 a.m.

Outside the cemetery office was a phone booth. He had plenty of dimes. And no more foolish pride.

However, the phone numbers he'd written on a scrap of paper kept in his wallet—one for a former teaching colleague, one for the home of the art history department chair at Marymount, numbers for his two cousins in Long Beach, the work number for a childhood friend now employed at a bakery in West LA, the office numbers of the trio of PI's he'd sequentially hired after Kyoko's murder—all had been blurred to inky gibberish by the soaking he'd gotten in the rain the night before.

And when he dialed 1-1-3 for information he was told there were no such listings.

He drove his car to the far end of the cemetery and parked it beneath a willow that hung over the narrow road.

All he knew was that nothing made sense.

So he had to make sense of that . . .

He had observed his mother lose her mind over the past few years. Though still only in her sixties, she had developed early senility that began with her forgetting details dating back a few weeks or months. Next, the memory loss encroached on her recent days, then her hours, then her minutes. Now, she couldn't say what she'd had for lunch, ten minutes after finishing. Nonetheless, she still recalled her distant past. Sumida as a child. . . . The death at age three of Sumida's sister, Yukiko, his only sibling, from Rheumatic Fever. . . . Her husband, Sam's father, as a young man (she thought he was still alive, not remembering he'd drowned off Dana Point). . . . Her girlhood in Japan. . . .

It was a plague of forgetfulness, leaving her only with the present moment and the distant past. No in-between.

And it was more than that.

At times, he'd observed his mother filling-in the blank spaces with delusions. For example, sometimes she believed she was being held captive, rather than being cared for, by her sister and brother-in-law—lashing out at them with profanity she had never used before. Sometimes she turned upon them with physical violence, clawing and scratching at their faces or throwing objects about the house. Other times she believed she was staying at a lodge in Yosemite and couldn't understand why she wasn't allowed to go outside alone to enjoy the pine trees and majestic views. Her sister would tell her it was because of an infestation of bears and that all the "guests" were required to stay inside for their own safety. Lies like that helped.

Sumida didn't like seeing such things. She was his mother, after all.

But he couldn't help being fascinated by the force of the delusions. More powerful than dreams, from which one can usually awaken oneself if the dream becomes too harrowing, these were alternative worlds from which she could not awake. Doctors referred to it as a form of senile psychosis.

It worried Sumida that his closest living relative suffered from such a thing. Particularly as he knew his paternal grandfather had suffered a similar psychological decline in Japan before his death in the 1890s. So now he couldn't help wondering . . .

Was it possible to skip the memory-loss portion of the illness and go straight to the psychosis?

Or would one even remember the memory-loss portion?

What other than madness made sense of all this? Sure, the driver's license in his wallet attested to his name and address. But the world objected. Still, this *had* to be different than his mother's affliction.

Everything depended on that being so.

Then he wondered: If Kyoko Sumida was not buried here, might that mean she was alive?

Was he still even investigating a murder?

He turned his car around and drove out of the cemetery, passing through the broken-down parts of Boyle Heights, where he'd have been beaten senseless even before America went to war with Japan, and back toward downtown.

The Hall of Records.

The newspaper files at the LA public library.

He was investigating a crime, for God's sake. His job was to get to the bottom of things.

❧

Excerpt from a letter dated August 1, 1942:

. . . Your reluctance is surely understandable, considering how recent events have affected you and your family. You have my sympathies. Indeed, if you were not off to such a good start with your Jimmy Park character, if I did not think you were truly onto something successful and new here, I'd agree that perhaps a more conventional approach to writing a mystery (i.e. a Caucasian protagonist working to solve an ordinary murder case) would be the way to go. But remember, it was the exciting prospect of doing a mystery novel from the point-of-view of an Oriental detective that initially drew me to your manuscript, distinguishing your work from other submis-

sions on the "slush pile." Your concept
of a Japanese protagonist grabbed me. And,
while geopolitical circumstances have
changed dramatically since that first submission, I do not believe we betray our
original intention to create something NEW
by having made the changes we have made to
this point.

Naturally, I do not want you to go forward
with something that makes you uncomfort-
able. But these are complex times. And you
are a young man, just starting out.

The truth is, there may be no better way
to introduce an Oriental as protagonist in
a popular spy story than the one afforded
us now: by making Park's enemy Japanese you
win over a mass audience's sympathies in a
way that your original plan to have your
Nisei detective solve the murder of his
wife by tracking down a Caucasian police
detective would never have accomplished.
The specter of "the Yellow Peril," like
it or not, might have doomed our project
even <u>before</u> Pearl Harbor. In fact, it now
seems reckless, almost mad, to have entertained the notion that we could pull that
off. So, mightn't the current revisions be
a blessing in disguise?

As I've said before, I don't mean to
offend by failing to acknowledge the dif-
ferences between Japanese and Koreans
(Chinese too, for that matter). I know
better than to lump all Orientals together.
And, for that reason, I understand that
for you this project may hold complex-
ities that most authors do not have to
face. But I recommend courage! The fact is,

there <u>are</u> Japanese spy rings in California, true? At least, there might be . . . So why <u>shouldn't</u> a Korean-American detective work to break them up? Think long about your answer to that question. While I do not for a moment believe you harbor Japanese Imperialist sympathies, I wonder if your hesitation to use Jimmy Park as your hero does not represent the very prejudice that you so eloquently derided in your most recent letter to me?

Look, I am a woman working as an editor of detective fiction—my office is dominated by men. I, too, know about being the underdog. And that is why I believe we make such a good team. The way to beat the system, my young friend, is to come up with some new approach to it. I believe that is exactly what you're doing with your book. So please weigh your decision carefully. Know that I will understand if you choose to cast your good beginning aside and write poetry or political tracts or whatever you choose. But know too that I <u>hope</u> I've persuaded you to continue your work on the book and that I am looking forward to receiving the next chapters.

Sincerely,

Maxine Wakefield
Maxine Wakefield,
Associate Editor,
Metropolitan Modern Mysteries, Inc.

P.S. This book could be big! And wouldn't that be a blessing for your family, especially there at Manzanar?

❧

Excerpt from chapter six of *The Orchid and the Secret Agent*, a novel by William Thorne
  Metropolitan Modern Mysteries, Inc., New York, N.Y., 1945

After a forty-minute car ride, Jimmy Park was guided out of the car, still blindfolded, and led fifty yards up a gravel path. While he could see nothing, his other senses remained acute. He smelled a hint of pine, mixed with the gasoline-tinged scent of the city, suggesting that he was in the foothills of the San Gabriel Mountains, perhaps Altadena or Sierra Madre. He heard birdsong and the crunch of the gravel underfoot. The men holding his arms stopped. Standing between them he turned to the agent on his right and sniffed, "Hmmm, Old Spice cologne," he said. Turning to the agent on his left he sniffed again. "No cologne, but a hint of Burma Shave." Neither agent responded, but a key turned in a lock and a heavy metal door opened. Inside, they continued down a corridor that smelled of metal and mildly mildewed drywall. Through another door, they passed into a room that featured thick carpeting and smelled of furniture oil, cigarettes, scotch whiskey, and (of all things!) orchids. Pressed down by his shoulders onto a leather chair, Jimmy reached for his blindfold, at last encountering no resistance. He tore it off.

For a moment, the light stung his eyes.

Before him was a large desk.

Seated behind the desk was a grey-haired man with sparkling blue eyes and a manner that seemed at once sophisticated and fire-hardened. He smiled at Jimmy, then stood (quite tall) and extended his hand across the desk.

Jimmy stood and shook his hand. "Mr. Barratt, I presume."

He nodded. "It's a pleasure to meet you Mr. Park. Please sit down."

Jimmy sat.

Mr. Barratt moved away from his big, leather swivel chair and came around to the front of the desk, leaning casually against one edge, like a friend or confidant rather than a professional superior. "I apologize for the blindfold, Mr. Park. Believe me, it was strictly for your protection."

"You mean in the event I'm captured by the Jap spy ring," Jimmy said.

"That's right."

Jimmy grinned. "So that no matter how much they torture me I'll be unable to tell them your location."

Mr. Barratt shrugged. "That's right too."

"Thanks for the 'protection,'" Jimmy said, good-naturedly.

Mr. Barratt laughed. "Yes, it's quite a line of work we've embarked upon, eh?"

Jimmy was gratified that Mr. Barratt referred to it as a shared line of work. It hadn't been that long since Park had worked as an ordinary PI, tracking down runaway daughters and shadowing unfaithful wives and husbands. The importation of Oriental criminal organizations these past few years had changed all that.

"The dashing out of the man's brains in the movie house," Mr. Barratt started, "the decapitation and quartering of your informant in the alley, the slashed throat of your neighbor . . . can't have been easy for you."

"No, sir."

"I would understand if you feel you've had enough of dealing with these people. If you'd prefer to withdraw from operations."

"But I haven't even begun to deal with 'these people!'" Jimmy answered.

"Good man!"

Jimmy looked around the room. It was windowless and paneled in fine, dark walnut, though at two or three places, where the wall met the plaster ceiling, he caught sight of cement beneath the paneling. He suspected this room was as much bunker as office. Nonetheless, it was comfortable. One wall was lined with crowded bookshelves and on the other wall hung a pair of large maps—one of Southern California, the other of the west coast of the United States. A conference table large enough to seat ten occupied most of the far end of the room and a door, half-ajar, led to a bathroom.

On the desk an arm's length away was a magnificent orchid.

"You're an orchid fancier?" Jimmy asked.

Mr. Barratt shook his head. "The flower's there as a reminder of what we're up against. It's of the Cymbidium variety, beautiful but poisonous."

Jimmy waited for further explanation.

"Don't worry, you'll understand soon enough," Mr. Barratt said. "Perhaps more than you ever wanted to."

Jimmy nodded—there was indeed a lot about this he didn't understand. But he suspected Mr. Barratt was unlikely to be rushed by questioning.

"Look, you've done an excellent job of getting the Jap organization's attention," Mr. Barratt said. "The enemy is, shall we say, 'engaged.'"

Jimmy nodded. "So far all the casualties have been on our side."

Mr. Barratt shrugged. "Indeed unfortunate. But . . . not altogether out of keeping with our plan."

"What?" Jimmy snapped.

"Jimmy, you've done good work for your country the past few years. We know how effective you've been infiltrating the Tong gangs, heading off massacres of Chinese-on-Chinese and even Chinese-on-whites! Your skills have made you invaluable. And impersonating a Yakuza crime lord was masterful and highly effective."

"Thank you, sir."

"And with the outbreak of war a few weeks ago, you became more important than ever," Mr. Barratt continued.

"Glad to hear it, sir."

"But Jimmy, there's a reason you're not in the FBI offices now, receiving a new assignment. The same reason you're here instead, at a top-secret installation."

"Yes, sir?"

Mr. Barratt tossed a photograph on the desk. "She's called the 'Orchid.' We don't know her actual name."

Jimmy picked up the picture.

"Study it," Mr. Barratt continued.

The woman was beautiful—her skin silk, her cheekbones and chin somehow imperially strong without diminishing the softness of her femininity, her black hair streaked with white.

"Look Jimmy, your success precedes you, not only here but among our enemies. You're *known* to these Jap spies. So obviously we can't use you anymore as an investigator."

Jimmy stood, agitated. "But sir, you can't leave me out of the fight."

"Please, sit," Mr. Barratt instructed.

Jimmy sat.

Mr. Barratt strode across the room to a portable bar set against the wall. He poured himself a rye.

"Drink, Jimmy?"

Jimmy nodded.

Mr. Barratt poured a second drink and then crossed the room back to Jimmy. He handed him the drink.

"To victory," Mr. Barratt toasted.

"Victory."

They drank.

"So tell me this, Jimmy. Now that your cover is essentially blown with the Jap infiltrators, how can you still be of service to your country?"

"Well," Jimmy started, thinking fast. But he didn't have a ready answer.

Mr. Barratt didn't wait for him to come up with one. "Don't strain, Jimmy. Let *me* tell you how you can serve."

Jimmy waited.

Mr. Barratt took a long drink before speaking. "All of the gruesome murders of the last twenty-four hours were either discovered by you, or, in the case of your quartered and decapitated informant, Gypsy Martinez, involved an important professional acquaintance. However, Jimmy, I don't believe they were intended as any sort of 'warning' to you."

"What else could they be?" Jimmy asked.

"These people don't 'warn' their victims," Mr. Barratt said. "They just kill them."

Jimmy shrugged. "So what are you thinking?"

"The killings were an invitation to you."

"Invitation? To me? For what?" Agitated, he didn't wait for an answer. "To go over to their side? To be some sort of double agent? You know I'd die first, sir. It'd never happen!"

Mr. Barratt held up one hand. "Never say 'never,' Jimmy."

Jimmy considered. "You mean . . ." He stopped.

"Yes, it's a way in."

⁂

Excerpt from a letter dated September 11, 1942:

. . . so gratified that my words served to clarify things for you. You're a strong young man indeed.

I can't wait to see your next couple of chapters. My trusty blue pencil has felt neglected these past weeks with no new pages from you. I believe our working in this close manner through your first draft has been most effective, don't you?

Sincerely,

Maxine Wakefield

Maxine Wakefield,
Associate Editor,
Metropolitan Modern Mysteries, Inc.

P.S. Perhaps, in the context of your recent "crisis of conscience," this is not the most delicate time to make the following editorial comment, but it's been much on my mind: I think it important that you establish early in the manuscript that all

the action takes place during what is now
the rather short period between the bombing
of Pearl Harbor and the relocation of you
Japanese Americans to camps. After all,
wouldn't it be during this brief period that
your Japanese villains (who, by the way,
I'm getting quite anxious to meet) would
have greatest mobility and thereby pose the
greatest threat? Of course, you don't want
to begin the book too close to December 7
of last year, as the shock that befell the
nation would distract from the ready spirit
of Jimmy to get right on with his business.
Also, you want to leave enough time for a
Japanese spy ring to become fully estab-
lished and functional (though, of course,
we might assume the spies commenced their
planning before Pearl Harbor). In any case,
I'm thinking that the story, as written,
begins sometime around the third week in
January. That allows enough time for the
villains to have laid their evil groundwork and enough time for Jimmy to track
them down, infiltrate them, and finally show
them justice, all before the internment
of Japanese Americans can intrude on the
story to become a potential distraction
to what must be a triumphant and patriotic climax. So, I'm thinking your story,
which you've so cleverly plotted to take
place over a little more than a single day,
begins January 21, 22, 23 . . . Whichever
you pick. After all, it's your book. Just
so long as it takes place before the President's Executive Order of February 19th,
which would confuse matters regarding the
Japanese still on the streets. Cheers!

THE REVISED—CHAPTER FOUR

. . . wipe away all trivial fond records.

—William Shakespeare

To discern why his wife's grave had been moved and where he might find it now, to say nothing of how his own house in Echo Park had, seemingly, become the property of someone else, Sumida would begin his research at the LA Department of Public Records, which was located in a large granite building near the corner of Spring and Temple Streets. He parked his stolen car in an alley off First Street, where it was unlikely to be noticed by any police while he was inside doing his research.

He climbed the steps of the Hall of Records, passed through a nine-foot-tall revolving door, and crossed to the information desk at the center of a crowded, marble lobby.

"Death records?" he asked.

A woman answered without looking up. "Birth and death, second floor," she said, doubtless for the ten-thousandth time.

Sumida was glad she hadn't looked up, glad she hadn't asked his name, glad she hadn't given him what would likely have been the same long, angry glare he'd seen more often these past twelve hours than in all the previous years of his life. However, he wasn't so lucky on the second floor, where, after passing through a pair of swinging glass doors, he arrived at a tall counter that divided Sumida from what seemed a city block filled with rows of shelves and filing cabinets. There, he was greeted by a scowling man in his fifties: "What do you want?"

"Death records," Sumida answered, placing his driver's license on the counter.

"Why, you kill somebody?" the grey-haired man asked as he read the name on the license.

Sumida grinned at the distasteful joke.

"Well?" the clerk pressed, scowling. "Did you? Kill somebody?"

"I just want to look into some records."

"Okay, I guess since you're not currently on one of the islands killing American Marines, maybe you haven't killed anybody, lately . . . 'course, if you *were* out there in the Pacific we both know which side you'd be fighting for, right?" He didn't wait for an answer. "Oh yeah, you'd be blasting away at the brave sons of this country, fueled by your rations of one goddamn bowl of rice per day, dug into your hole like the vermin you people are . . ."

Sumida picked up his license and started away.

"And yet you've got the gall to walk into a United States government building," the man continued, almost shouting after him. "Looking for assistance from real Americans, white, employed Americans, who are here now instead of in the Pacific only because we're all either women or old men like me, and you ask us to do you a clerical service just because you got yourself a goddamn California driver's license or whatever it is you think you got that can prove you belong here . . ."

The man at the desk kept talking, even after Sumida turned a corner and was out of sight.

Ten minutes later, after calming his anger and gathering his resolve by splashing cold water on his face in a deserted men's room down the hall, Sumida returned to the desk.

The grey-haired man was gone, perhaps someplace among the stacks of records. Sumida approached a woman whose platinum blonde hair and shapeless dress seemed ten years behind the times. He asked her the same question.

"Death records?"

This time, it went better.

Until, that is, she returned a few minutes later and said, "Sorry, but we don't have what you're looking for."

"You must."

"I checked twice."

"Look, did that grey-haired man tell you to . . ." he started.

"No," she interrupted. "I'm sorry about him, too. I heard how he spoke to you. But his son was killed last week on the Bataan Peninsula. This is Mr. Wilson's first day back. Obviously, he's not ready. So he's in the break room now, composing himself. You won't see him again. And no . . . he offered no interference to my record search. I was thorough."

"But you found nothing."

"That's right."

"That's impossible."

"It's the truth."

There were no records of Kyoko Sumida's death on January 11, 1941? No record of her death at all, anytime? Momentarily, this filled Sumida with the same irrational exuberance he'd experienced at the cemetery when it had occurred to him (despite his having *personally* identified her body in the LA Coroner's Office) that perhaps Kyoko wasn't actually dead. But there were also no records of her birth in Santa Monica on June 8, 1911. And no record of their marriage at the LA City Hall, just up the street, in 1934.

"Look Miss, what about a Satoki Samuel Sumida?"

"Can you spell that?"

He did.

"What kind of record?" she asked.

"Birth certificate."

"Satoki Samuel Sumida is you?"

He nodded and showed her his driver's license.

She jotted down information on a notepad. "And you were born in this county?"

"LA County General. You need the date?"

"No, I noted your birthday here off your license."

She turned and again disappeared among the shelves and tall cabinets.

He put his license away. As the minutes passed, he grew increasingly certain of what she was going to say to him, even though it would make no more sense than anything else she'd said.

"I'm afraid we have no record for your birth in this county," she said. "Are you sure you were born here?"

"Of course."

She looked at him.

He observed the expression on her face change. A subtle widening of the eyes, a slight inhalation of breath, a false pursing of her lips in order to try to pull it all back together. "Perhaps I should get my supervisor," she managed to say, waiting for no response before turning and walking with self-conscious ease toward the back.

Sumida considered what it must look like to her: a Japanese man claiming to be Nisei with no record of local birth. . . . He suspected it was at least as likely that she was dialing the police right now as that she was seeking out her supervisor.

With no rational explanation to offer to authorities, he knew better than to wait.

He turned and exited through the glass double doors, descending the staircase to the marble foyer, through which he continued outside. On the crowded sidewalk, he wondered: Would there have been a death certificate for his father? Or his sister, who'd died in this country as a child? Maybe he should have stayed and asked.

But he felt he already knew the answer—though he'd no clue, beyond the possibility of his own insanity, to the *why* of it all.

Still, he was determined not to give up.

The library was a fifteen-minute walk. There, he'd request a copy of the newspaper from January 12, 1941, which had featured a story on page eight of the News section about the discovery of his wife's body in the San Pedro Harbor. From the library, the *LA Times* building was a mere Ben Hogan tee shot away; Sumida would contact the reporter who wrote the story (whose name eluded him now). Perhaps the newspaperman, sensing a good story, might partner with Sumida to help unravel the confusions of the last few hours. With neither a home, nor a car, nor, apparently, an identity recognizable to *anyone*, he was begin-ning to think he needed the help of a stranger.

When he walked by the alley where he'd left the Chrysler, he spied a cop surveying the car.

Well, there's no percentage to driving around in the stolen car of an LAPD sergeant, anyway, Sam thought, continuing past the alley like any passerby and toward the city's main library. He was glad he'd taken the .38 Special out of the car with him.

Twenty minutes later, in the periodicals room, he handed over his library card and drummed his fingers on the desk while he waited for the particular back issue of the *Times* to be retrieved. January 12, 1941 . . . A woman with a gold comb in her hair, like Linda Darnell wore in *The Mark of Zorro*, returned from a back room with the newspaper.

She gave it to him.

He was tempted to tip her simply for having made no derogatory comments about his race. But a library was no place for tips. And, as he had only $6.34 in his possession, he was in no position to give any-thing away.

He took the paper to a chair near a high window that gave good light.

The front page looked as he remembered it.

But there was nothing about Kyoko's murder on page eight. Instead, stories about a local beauty contest, charges of tax fraud against the Riverside city manager, and ads for a car dealership and a bedding store.

There was nothing about Kyoko on page nine or ten or any other page.

Sumida returned the newspaper to the woman with the Linda Darnell comb.

"Thank you," she said, handing back his library card in exchange. "It's funny. But another gentleman asked to see that same edition just a few minutes ago."

"January 12th?"

She nodded. "A tall man in a nicely cut suit," she continued. "He returned the edition and asked for other dates." She looked away, as if remarking to herself. "Quite a handsome man, actually."

"Is he in this room?" Sumida asked, looking around.

"I assume he is." She looked around, too. "After all, one's not allowed to take periodicals from here."

Four or five men and a trio of women were scattered about the seating area, hidden behind open newspapers.

Then one of the men closed and folded his paper.

After doing so, his eyes went straight to Sumida's.

It was Lieutenant Henry Czernicek, who had headed the LAPD investigation of Kyoko's murder. The one who'd done so little to solve the crime . . .

"Yes, he's the one who asked for January 12th," the woman said.

Sumida held Czernicek's gaze.

At last, the detective stood. "Sumida?" he called across the room.

"You recognize me?" Sam asked, starting toward Czernicek.

"Of course, and you . . . you recognize *me*?" the police detective asked, his manner uncharacteristically diffident.

There weren't many men outside of the movies who looked like Czernicek, whose strong chin, piercing blue eyes, and ramrod straight posture set him apart from every other plainclothesman in the squad room (though the good looks and hardboiled manner belied, at best, a merely ordinary intelligence, Sumida believed). "Czernicek," Sumida answered.

They met in the middle of the room but didn't shake hands.

"What are you doing here?" Sumida asked.

"Research. You?"

"Same."

"What are you researching, Sumida?"

"My past."

"Yeah, why?"

How to answer without sounding mad? But there was little point in just letting Czernicek walk away. He alone had recognized Sumida. That was no small thing. "Strange things have been happening to me since last night," Sumida said, lowering his voice. "Or maybe the strange things have been happening to the world, I don't know which. I know *I* haven't changed, right? You can see that for yourself. But . . ." He hesitated. In

Sumida's view, the taciturn Czernicek had failed in his investigation of Kyoko's murder in part because of an innate lack of imagination (to say nothing of his lack of motivation). So what would the plainclothesman make now of Sumida's irrational tale of the last eighteen hours? He'd probably put Sumida away in Camarillo. "Anyway, despite our disagreements in the past, I'm relieved to see you here."

Czernicek nodded. "Me too."

Sumida couldn't leave it at that. "At the risk of sounding a note of 'strangeness,'" he said, "I'm relieved that you, well . . . recognize me." He expected to be asked to elaborate.

But that's not what Czernicek did.

"Yeah, the feeling's kind of mutual," the plainclothesman said. "Something funny's been going on."

"Since last night?" Sumida asked.

Czernicek nodded. "I've taken a hotel room not too far from here."

"Hotel room?"

Czernicek lowered his voice to a whisper. "Yeah, it turns out my apartment is occupied by someone who claims he's been there for years. And my landlord backs him up. In fact, the landlord says he *never* rented to me, never even saw me before. Of course, he's lying. Got to be. . . . Though for the life of me I can't figure the scam. Except . . ."

"What?" Sumida pressed.

"Well, until now, *no one* has seemed to recognize me," Czernicek answered, fiddling with the knot of his tie. "Not even at the precinct, where all the guys . . ."

He was interrupted by the librarian with the Linda Darnell comb, who'd come out from behind her desk. "I'm sorry, gentlemen. But this is no place for a conversation. Quiet is the rule around here."

Both men nodded apologies.

"Follow me, Sumida," Czernicek said. "Maybe we can figure this out together."

Czernicek may have failed to solve Kyoko's murder months before, and he'd never been among Sam's favorite people, but he might yet prove useful.

Besides, it felt good to be called by name—better yet not to be alone.

❧

Excerpt from chapter seven of *The Orchid and the Secret Agent*, a novel by William Thorne
    Metropolitan Modern Mysteries, Inc., New York, N.Y., 1945

. . . Mr. Barratt interrupted the three-star Army general, Walter Stark, who sat across from him at the far end of the conference table in Barratt's secret office, bunkered in the foothills of the San Gabriel Mountains.

"*Of course* there's no record of the existence of the Orchid!" Mr. Barratt snapped, slapping his palm on the table. "But that doesn't mean she's not the woman behind this brutal syndicate, whatever your Army Intelligence agent reports!"

Jimmy sat at Mr. Barratt's right, a position of honor.

What Jimmy had done to deserve such a position was a mystery to him—unless it had more to do with what he was about to be asked to do.

That worried him a bit. But he'd volunteered to do anything to help the cause.

He looked around the table.

Filling out the places were a Marine Corps colonel, a Naval Intelligence officer, an air corps colonel, two FBI supervisors, representatives from the State, Treasury, and War Departments, the police commander in charge of counterintelligence for the city of Los Angeles, Barrett, General Stark, and a United States senator.

"Look, just because you've got the President's ear doesn't mean you can talk to me with that tone, Barratt," General Stark answered.

"That's Mr. Barratt to you, General."

The general ignored him. "Your 'secret' Secret Service, or whatever you want to call it, may prove an effective way to pull intelligence from our various agencies together, but that doesn't mean the intelligence your people gather is better than what we get. And so I want to know how you learned this dragon lady's known as the Orchid when none of the rest of us has been able to find any such evidence."

The others at the table turned to Mr. Barratt, who took a long, slow breath. "We also suspect that she may have a personal bodyguard, likely a martial arts expert of unsurpassed skill whose face has never been seen by anyone who lived to describe it. We've managed to compile no facts about him, beyond his being known as *Fantomu*, which translates as 'Phantom.'"

"Damn it man, stay on this 'Dragon Lady,'" the general insisted. "Codename Orchid. This is about intelligence sharing, right?"

Most of the other men at the table nodded, silently.

"Do you know what *seppuku* is, General Stark?" Mr. Barratt asked, calmly.

"It means 'suicide' in Japanese," General Stark answered.

"Not quite so simple," Mr. Barratt responded. "It is a *form* of suicide, highly ritualized and dating back to the days of the Samurai warriors. Considered an honorable way to end one's own life, it involves self-disembowelment with a short knife called a *tanto*, which is ripped across the lower gut. Usually, the practitioner of *seppuku* has a 'second' who, after the intestines spill into the open, uses a sword to decapitate the suicide, relieving him of his suffering."

"I didn't come here for lessons in Jap culture," General Stark responded. "And you're not answering my question!"

"Please, gentlemen," the senator said, holding his open palms in the air. "We're all on the same side here." He turned to Mr. Barratt. "Continue as you see fit, but do not neglect the general's question."

"As you wish," Mr. Barratt said.

Jimmy felt his face grow hot with the tension and sense of high stakes in the room.

"Our last agent infiltrated the Orchid's organization for less than a single day," Mr. Barratt said, his voice steady. "Unfortunately, he was found out and, we can assume from the remaining evidence, that he was offered the choice between torture and *seppuku*. I don't have to tell you how gifted the Japanese are at inflicting torture. So, naturally, he chose *seppuku*. His body, discovered last week in a downtown warehouse near Saint Vibiana's, indicates that he indeed sliced deeply across his own belly from hip bone to hip bone. But the Jap bastards denied him the sword, leaving him instead to die a slow, painful death, gagged and bound at the feet, alone in a pitch-dark room. But they underestimated our man, who, after all, was an American and capable of a strength of spirit that they could not imagine. In his final moments he used his own blood and guts, and I mean that quite literally, to write the 'The Orchid,' on his own bare chest. And that, General Stark and distinguished gentlemen, is how we came to know the name of our nemesis."

The men around the table sat silent.

Even General Stark wiped at a line of sweat on his forehead.

"And so, thanks to this patriot, we know more now than we knew before," the senator observed. "She is the Orchid, for whom no records exist."

"Yes," Mr. Barratt said.

"Fine, but without records what use is that to us?" the senator pressed. "You've discerned assumed names. So what? The question remains, what are we going to do about it now?"

Mr. Barratt turned to Jimmy. "We have a new way in."

"Jimmy Park . . ." the Marine Corps colonel muttered, doubtfully.

"If you have doubts, please express them directly," Mr. Barratt requested of the colonel.

The Marine looked directly at Jimmy and shook his head disdainfully. "An Oriental is going to come through for our nation where the best of Army and Navy Intelligence have failed? No offense, young man, but I have my doubts."

Jimmy straightened in his chair, speaking for the first time. "As a matter of fact, sir, I *will* come through for our nation."

"I wish I could believe you," the Marine Corps colonel said.

Jimmy nodded as if sympathizing. Then he smiled. After a moment, he pushed back his chair and stood.

The distinguished contingent watched silently.

Jimmy crossed the paneled room to Mr. Barratt's desk. He reached for the beautiful but deadly Cymbidium orchid that Barratt had said he kept as a reminder of his nemesis. Jimmy grabbed the stem up near the purple bloom and snapped it off. Returning to the table, he dropped the bloom onto the table.

"This is how I will deliver her up, gentlemen."

Excerpt from a letter dated October 16, 1942:

. . . you've figured out by now that I con- sider the selection of names for characters to be an integral part of characterization (not everything, of course, but not "nothing" either). However, while I found your scene with the gathered Intelligence officers in Mr. Barratt's office to be riveting, I must admit to having been distracted by the mul- titude of names you introduced. As a result, I've taken my blue pencil to the manuscript, eliminating most of the names. I think that with the exception of the Army general, Mr. Barratt's most vocal challenger, all the others gathered around that conference table are just as well referred to simply by their titles. Additionally, I think that since we're in Jimmy's POV these cuts are further justified, as he'd not catch every name but would surely be aware of their pow- erful positions.

On another note, I noticed the name you gave to the Marine colonel in your draft was "Czernicek." Of course, there's no refer- ence to his first name being "Henry." None- theless, while the name "Henry Czernicek" worked well in your initial (now discarded) synopsis and opening chapters as a mur-

derous LAPD officer, I didn't like seeing
it used again in another context. I have a
pet peeve about discarded characters' names
being interchangeable with other, subsequent characters. You may think of it as my
personal quirk. Don't get me wrong. I love
that you recycled some elements of your
original concept into this draft, such as
the location of the bungalow in Echo Park,
the '37 Dodge, and even a few characters,
such as Tony Fortuna. And I don't mind that
you used the same description, literally
word-for-word, of the Orchid's appearance
as you used to describe poor Kyoko Sumida
in the first chapter of your abandoned Jap-
anese-hero novel. It's a pretty face you
sketch for us, no doubt. Obviously, you're
attracted to a particular, if conventional,
kind of beauty. No problem. But I draw the
line at reassigning to this work the names
of characters <u>cut</u> from the original manuscript, as I believe it demonstrates a
lack of specificity of imagination for your
current characters.

In any case, you keep creating at your
end and know that I anxiously await your
next chapters, blue pencil poised and ready!

Warmly,

Maxine Wakefield
Maxine Wakefield,
Associate Editor,
Metropolitan Modern Mysteries, Inc.

THE REVISED—CHAPTER FIVE

Can Providence have worked in any way other than to have
placed a single good man and a single unrepentant villain at
Christ's sides, reverse images of each other, bound together on Gol-
gotha by their isolation from the world they had known before?
—Sister Aimee Semple McPherson

"Have you eaten lunch?" Henry Czernicek asked Sumida as they emerged from the library onto Fifth Street.

"No."

"Hungry?"

The last thing Sumida remembered eating was a homemade dinner of fried eggs with toast before leaving his house to see *The Maltese Falcon* at the Rialto Movie House. Was that early last night? Or was it almost two months ago? In either case, eating hadn't occurred to him in the interim. But now, with Czernicek at his side, he felt better. That one person recognized him, and an LAPD detective at that, was a world of difference from being recognizable to *no one*. He felt almost cheerful. "I could stand to eat a sandwich," he answered.

"I know a good diner a couple of blocks away, just on the other side of Pershing Square near that Italian fruit stand," Czernicek said, starting in that direction.

Sumida caught up.

"Funny, you and me again," Czernicek continued as they neared the Biltmore Hotel, which was bustling with men in uniform, and continued on past the Philharmonic Hall, where Sumida had once taken Kyoko to see Vladimir Horowitz.

"Yeah, funny. Or something," Sumida answered.

Their parting a few months before had not been friendly. Sam had believed, initially, that the LAPD would devote whatever manpower and effort was necessary to solve the murder of his wife. But he'd been naïve. After the investigation ruled out the most likely suspect—Sam himself—the department had seemed to lose interest. That was just a few days after the crime, when real police work would be necessary. Subsequently, the LAPD managed only to dig up a few sordid details about the last months of Sam and Kyoko's marriage. She'd been seen in various downtown hotels with a Caucasian man, though none of the front desk clerks at the hotels could offer any descriptions of the man. Sumida had been under the impression that this was the sort of information cops beat out of uncooperative witnesses, "helping" them to remember. But there were no beatings—no one even taken to the station. So there were no artist's renderings of the Caucasian lover displayed in newspapers as part of a dragnet. Czernicek himself pointed out to Sumida that even if they tracked down the man she'd been seeing they still might not have the actual murderer. A lead, perhaps . . . But most leads go nowhere. And when, three weeks into the investigation, the case had slipped so far down the list of active investigations that Sam no longer got his phone calls put through or returned, he waited one day outside Central Station for Czernicek and confronted the much-bigger man, offering a list of grievances that arose as much from his broken heart as from his disillusionment with the shoddy police work. Czernicek admitted then that finding the killers of Japs or Chinks was only a little higher up the list of police priorities than finding the killers of Mexicans or Negroes. Sam took a swing, which the plainclothesman sidestepped. Czernicek had laughed and said he could put Sam behind bars for attempting to assault an officer but would settle instead for Sumida's agreement to spare the department his demands and move on with his life, accepting that *most crimes are never solved*. That's when Sam had emptied his bank account to hire the first of a string of equally ineffective PIs. He hadn't seen Czernicek again.

Until today.

And now they were lunching together. Funny . . .

Funnier yet was that Czernicek was the only acquaintance Sumida had in the world. Ha-ha.

"Get the pastrami," Czernicek said, after they'd taken seats at the booth farthest from the counter, cash register, and crowd.

The waitress, a nineteen or twenty-year-old looker in a hairnet and mustard-stained uniform, followed on their heels, stopping at their booth with one fist placed coquettishly against her hip. "Sorry, but we don't serve Japs."

Sumida looked away.

"This man's name is Chan," Czernicek said. "He's Chinese."

She looked doubtful.

Czernicek removed his badge from his suit jacket pocket and showed it to her. "You can trust me, little flower."

"Oh, well that's okay then." She removed her order pad from a big pocket on her uniform and a pencil from within her nest of blonde hair. "What can I get for you and your *friend*, Officer?"

"My friend's first name is Charlie," Czernicek said.

It took the waitress a moment to make the connection. "Charlie Chan?" Doubt crossed her face like a shadow.

"And my name's Henry Czernicek, LAPD," he said.

"Okay, fine," she said. "You know what you want to order?"

"Two pastrami sandwiches and coffee," Czernicek answered, putting his ID back in his suit jacket pocket.

She returned her pencil to her hair and put her order pad into the pocket of her uniform.

"Aren't you a doll?" Czernicek said to her as she turned to go.

She turned back, looking over her shoulder, mustering teenaged allure. "Thanks for the compliment, Detective."

"Detective *what*?" Czernicek quizzed her.

She stopped. "Your name?"

"Yeah, I just told you, little doll."

She shrugged. "Henry . . . something."

"Good enough," Czernicek said.

"Okay," she said, confused.

"You can put our order in now," Czernicek instructed.

She sashayed away.

"Charlie Chan?" Sumida asked him.

Czernicek said nothing, but watched the waitress go. Then he reached across the table and, without warning, grabbed Sumida's wrist, twisting it hard until Sumida thought it might break.

"Tell me what the hell is going on," Czernicek demanded.

"I don't know."

He twisted harder.

Sumida fixed Czernicek with a glare, even as tears formed unbidden in his eyes.

Czernicek twisted harder still.

Sumida could reach across the table with his free hand and hit the big cop in the head with the metal napkin dispenser, opening a hole in his skull. He knew after what he'd done last night in his own bungalow in Echo Park that he was more capable of inflicting physical damage than he'd believed.

But what would that accomplish now?

So instead he just held Czernicek's glare, daring the big man to twist his wrist clean off.

At last, Czernicek let go.

"Okay, Sumida, so you don't know what's going on either. We're partners then. But if this is some kind of trick . . ."

Sumida dropped his sore wrist onto his lap, cradling it beneath the table. "That's how it works being partners with you, Czernicek?"

"I just needed to know you weren't in on something."

Sumida laughed. "Me, in on something? I'm on the outside of everything, barely even looking in. You understand? Since last night . . . And, I suspect, since a long time before that. So don't test me again, you son of a bitch."

Czernicek grinned. "Yeah, this is going to be a real fun partnership."

With his good hand, Sumida took a drink of water. "Tell me what happened when you went to the precinct."

Czernicek shrugged. "Everybody there acted like they didn't know me."

"'Acted' like they didn't know you or . . . didn't *know* you?"

"Yeah, that's the question, Hamlet," Czernicek said. "Do I be or don't I be?"

Sumida was surprised that Czernicek was capable of playfully appropriating Shakespeare. And he was disturbed by the appropriation—it was more than merely playful. It was the same question he'd been asking himself.

But didn't their recognizing one another put it to rest?

Why did it feel to Sumida like the answer might still be no?

"Of course, stranger yet was that I didn't recognize any of them," Czernicek said as he mindlessly picked out sugar cubes, one at a time, from a porcelain container next to the salt and paper shakers, lining the cubes in rows of six, parallel to the edge of the Formica tabletop before him. "Still, I walked across the homicide department toward my office, greeting these imposters as if they were compadres. At first, they ignored me, confused. When I got to my office door I found my name wasn't on it anymore. That's when two of them grabbed me by the arms and threw me out like I was some kind of crazy civilian. I'll get the bastards, in time. You can count on that. But first I got to figure out what's going on."

Sumida nodded.

"What about you?" Czernicek asked.

Sumida reviewed his own facts from the last eighteen hours, starting with the breaking of the film at the movie house. Of course, he left a few things out of his story. Like his visit to his home in Echo Park, where, according to the morning news on the car radio, Tony Fortuna had been killed. Who was to say that Czernicek wasn't putting all this on just to get him to confess to the crime? And Sumida also left out his visit to the cemetery, as he didn't want to bring up Kyoko's name— not with the man who'd considered her insufficiently important to take finding her killer seriously. Sumida couldn't afford to get tangled up in that resentment again. Not when Czernicek seemed his best hope to figure out what was happening. But he told Czernicek about his parking claim check at the downtown lot being two months old and about his aunt and uncle's house now being occupied by strangers.

"I was sitting in a coffee shop last night reading a book," Czernicek said. "Hemingway's new one, *For Whom the Bell Tolls*. I'd just bought it at Williams' Book Store in San Pedro. Not even ten pages in . . ."

"I wouldn't have pegged you for a reader," Sumida interrupted.

Czernicek glared at him.

"Being a man of action, I mean," Sumida added.

"There's plenty of action in Hemingway," Czernicek observed. Then he returned to lining up the sugar cubes in rows. "Suddenly, the lights in the coffee shop flicker. And then all the electricity goes out. Blackness. Even outside through the big picture windows. No moonlight, starlight, nothing. Just like you describe in the movie house. Only for a second or two. And when the light comes back on I'm still sitting in the booth with the book in my hand, like nothing's changed, except that everybody in the place is different."

"Different?"

Czernicek began to stack the parallel lines of sugar cubes atop one another, forming a wall three or four inches high in front of him. "I mean a whole set of different people, at the counter and in the booths. And then my regular waitress, who's the reason I put up with the crap food at this place, comes over and asks for my order. As if she *ever* has to ask. Hell, I order the same thing every time I go there: chicken fried steak. Just like I always get the pastrami here. But now it's like she doesn't know that. And it's like she doesn't know *me*, which is exactly what she claims when I press her about it. Good God, I've taken that little girl to my bed a time or two after her shift and now she says she doesn't recognize me? So I lose my temper and make a scene and it's only by flashing my badge that things simmer down and I get out of there all right."

"But you're telling me things weren't all right, even after you got out of there."

"Yeah, that's what I'm telling you," Czernicek said, knocking over the sugar cube wall.

The waitress came with the sandwiches on plates in each hand.

Czernicek scooped up the sugar cubes and returned them to the porcelain bowl.

Sumida made a mental note not to take sugar with his tea if he ever returned to this place.

"Eat up," Czernicek said, as the waitress put down the food.

She turned and walked away.

"That one," Czernicek indicated, with a wave of his hand toward the retreating waitress. "She ought to know me too. And she sure as hell should know my last name. She lives at home and likes to fuck in her lacy little girlhood bedroom, not ten feet from her Mom and Dad's room. She likes me to put a pillow over her face when she starts making too much noise. And now, you see, she doesn't even recognize me."

Sumida shook his head. "You got a thing for waitresses, Czernicek?"

"I got a thing for women," he answered, biting into his sandwich. "But waitresses . . . Well, women who spend their whole working day on their feet are especially appreciative of a man who puts them flat on their backs."

Sumida grunted.

"But this isn't about that," Czernicek said.

"No."

"What's going on, Sumida? Are we ghosts or something?"

The thought had occurred to Sumida. He'd dismissed it. "I think these people would respond to us differently if that were the case," he answered.

"Then what's your theory, professor?"

Sumida picked up his sandwich with his good hand. He shrugged, *I don't know.*

"Hell of a lot of good running into you has done me," Czernicek said.

Sumida put his sandwich down. "Our recognizing each other means everything, however little we may understand what's going on."

"Oh, why?"

"Because it means we're not insane."

Czernicek laughed. "Was that worrying you?"

Sumida said nothing.

"Or maybe it's all a dream," Czernicek said.

Sumida shook his head. "You know that business about pinching yourself to ascertain that you're not dreaming?"

"Sure."

Sumida brought his sore wrist up from beneath the table, where he'd kept it resting on his lap.

It was already black and blue where Czernicek had twisted it.

"No dream," Sumida said.

Czernicek ignored his brutal handy work. "So that brings us back to our being ghosts."

Sumida shook his head. "I've been to the Hall of Records. There's no indication of my ever having existed. No birth certificate, marriage license, real estate or tax records . . . nothing. Ghosts leave behind *some* indication of their having once been alive."

"So what do you make of it, Sumida?"

Privately, Sumida suspected the two were not ghosts, but phantoms of another, even more disturbing order—beings who seemed never to have lived at all, despite their memories. Impossible, of course. "No clue," he answered.

"And why just you and me?" Czernicek wondered.

Sumida had already silently inventoried the areas of common ground between them. There was only one . . . Kyoko, who was absent in the public records. "I don't know, Czernicek. Maybe we're just meant for each other."

"Very funny."

Sumida wondered if this strange reunion was an opportunity to accomplish what they had not accomplished before? *To solve the crime?* Had the two men been singled out for this sudden, inexplicable isolation—more than that, their excision from the past—for just such a purpose, justice? There was nothing Sumida wanted more than to find his wife's killer; losing his house, his car, and his identity would prove a small price to pay if that was what setting things right required. But there remained the problem of how to begin such an investigation when there was no record of Kyoko's either being born, married, *or* murdered. . . .

Sumida kept all this to himself for now.

He suspected that Czernicek was not the sort of man with whom one could speculate about metaphysics, even in the midst of an inexplicable episode. And uninvited talk of the murder investigation (a contentious subject) would threaten this forced but useful partnership.

"And another thing," Czernicek continued, his frustration level increasing. "Along with everything else, I'm well aware of the suspicious 'coincidence' of our meeting this morning in the periodicals room."

Sumida looked at Czernicek. "I don't think our meeting was such a coincidence. We found ourselves in roughly the same situation, displaced. So it seems to me reasonable that we'd think to go to the same resource for some kind of 'catching-up.'"

Czernicek turned to Sumida. "Our situation might be similar. But what gives you the idea we think alike?"

Sumida said nothing.

"You're a dirty Jap," Czernicek whispered.

"I was born in this country, just like you," Sumida answered.

Czernicek laughed. "I was *born* in the Austro-Hungarian Empire. I came here as a kid. But *I'm* an American. A real one. And you're still a Jap."

"Go to hell, Czernicek."

Czernicek shook his head, fatalistically. Then, with the tip of his index finger, he poked the side of Sumida's head. "Hasn't it occurred to you that we may already *be* in hell?"

So, metaphysics wasn't beyond Czernicek . . . But Sumida disagreed with his appraisal. "This isn't hell."

Czernicek raised his chin. "How can you be so sure?"

"Because there're important things for us to do here."

Czernicek flashed his movie-star smile. "That's why I like you, Sumida," he said, slapping him on the shoulder. "Even with your squinty eyes and toothy grin and sneaky Oriental mind, you manage to hold out hope when there's none. Like with the murder of your wife . . . No solution. So you became a *private detective*? Ha! One optimistic Jap is what you are."

"*Keizoku wa chikara nari*," Sumida answered, knowing the Japanese would aggravate him. "It means 'perseverance is power.'"

"Spare me your Mr. Moto wise sayings," Czernicek chortled bitterly. "And let me amend how I described you a minute ago: you're not just one optimistic Jap, you're a downright gullible one."

"If you think I'm a joke, then you should go your own way," Sumida said. Though he knew that teaming with Czernicek was his best chance to figure out what was going on, he wouldn't be continually insulted.

Czernicek shook his head. "I need you like you need me. Christ, do you think I'd even be seen sitting here with you if I didn't?"

Sumida said nothing.

"Did you read about Pearl Harbor in the periodicals room this morning?" Czernicek asked.

Sumida shook his head. "That's not where I started." He'd started with the *Times* edition from the day after Kyoko's body was found. "But I heard a radio report and picked up the gist . . ."

"Not where you started?" Czernicek interrupted, disgust entering his voice. "It was a sneak attack, Sumida. No declaration of war. Just a lazy Sunday morning, like any other. Our Navy boys peaceably sleeping. You understand?" He didn't wait for an answer. "And then Jap aircraft descend and within a couple of hours there are thousands of Americans dead, all of them blown up or drowned or gunned down or burned. It's a goddamn world war, Sumida, and in the periodicals room it's not where you start? Is your kind even human?"

"I had nothing to do with Pearl Harbor," Sumida said.

"Yeah, well, it's going to have plenty to do with you," Czernicek snapped.

Sumida knew he was right about that.

"You haven't noticed the soldiers deployed all over LA?" Czernicek continued, not waiting for an answer. "The Chavez Ravine Naval Base, Fort MacArthur in San Pedro, Camp Roberts up north . . ."

jumping. Meantime, hundreds of the most suspicious Japs, both men and women, are incarcerated on Terminal Island or in the city jail or the Hall of Justice jail or the county lockups or wherever we got space for them. There's even talk that preparations are being made to move all your kind into camps up in the desert. And I mean *all*."

"I'm a loyal American," Sumida said.

"Yeah, you are. Problem is, that's what they all say."

"Maybe they're telling the truth," Sumida observed.

"Most probably are," Czernicek conceded. "But if even a handful . . . Well, better safe than sorry, right?"

Sumida said nothing.

"You know there's an eight p.m. curfew for Japs, right Sumida? You *do* know that."

Sumida said nothing. He'd heard plenty of references to it but lacked details.

"You should have done a better job in the periodicals room," Czernicek said.

"Whatever the circumstances, we're in this together, whether you like it or not," Sumida said.

"You're right. I don't like it. But what we like or don't like doesn't seem to count for much in this world. Or, for that matter, in the last world either." He leaned across the booth. "Go be a 'detective' on your own for a few hours, Sumida. Figure out what you can. Meet me at eight o'clock back at my hotel, The Barclay on Fourth and Main. You know it?"

Sumida nodded. "What's your plan?"

Czernicek looked at his watch. "I've got a few things to look into. Some broads I know who'd never forget me, by God. Then, come six o'clock I'll go back to police headquarters. With a little luck, there'll be someone coming onto the evening shift who either recognizes me or is careless enough that I can slip past him and into my office. I still have the key. Well, *a* key. Whether it works anymore . . ." He stopped.

"What do you expect to find there?"

"Maybe I'll find some evidence of my life or some clue as to what kind of scam this is."

Sumida suspected he'd simply find that the room was now someone else's office and had been for years. "You need my help?"

"How would you help?"

"A diversion."

Czernicek laughed. "No, Sumida." He spoke softly to insure no one could hear. "You're a Jap with California ID that matches up with *nothing* in the public record. You hear me? Look, you're no good to me being interrogated and then imprisoned and maybe executed as a spy."

Sumida hadn't allowed himself to fully consider what the authorities would make of his predicament.

Czernicek stood and slipped his hand into his pocket, removing a ten dollar bill. He dropped it on the table. "Take it."

Sumida looked at the money.

Unfortunately, he needed it. He took the sawbuck and slid out of the booth.

"I'll settle the bill for the pastrami up front," Czernicek said, starting toward the cash register. "But I don't want you standing next to me, understand? People are starting to take note. Wait for me in the square."

Sumida said nothing as he exited the diner.

It felt good to be in fresh air.

He crossed the street and sat at a wooden bench near the statue of General Pershing.

❧

Excerpt from chapter eight of *The Orchid and the Secret Agent*, a novel by William Thorne

Metropolitan Modern Mysteries, Inc., New York, N.Y., 1945

... It was now forty minutes since the senator, the men from Military Intelligence, and the LAPD commander of counterintelligence had exited Mr. Barratt's office, apparently satisfied that Jimmy was up to the risky assignment (or, at least, that he was sufficiently insignificant to sacrifice for the war effort in the event the operation failed). Now, Jimmy and Mr. Barratt entered what looked like a windowless classroom (but for an absence of school desks) that was located even deeper than Mr. Barratt's office in the bunker-like complex.

"This is it," Mr. Barratt said. "One of our code-breaking rooms."

Three young men, all attired in short-sleeved white dress shirts and black ties, all of them bespectacled and thin as rails, stood one each at three wall-length blackboards. None turned toward Jimmy and Mr. Barratt. They hadn't even seemed to notice the pair's entrance. Instead, each silently studied strings of English words written on the blackboard before him. One stared at his board with his chin in his hand; another stared while scratching distractedly at his head; the third stared as he rattled coins in his pants pockets. In all, the effect was of three younger and more respectably coiffed Einsteins studying formulae.

"Gentlemen," Mr. Barratt announced.

The three jumped, almost as one, startled by the sound of Mr. Barratt's voice.

"Sir!" they said, all snapping to attention (in a kind of sloppy, schoolboy fashion).

Mr. Barratt chuckled warmly. "I didn't mean to startle you, boys."

"No problem, sir," said one.

"Nor would I have interrupted your impressive and obviously focused attention on the work at hand," Mr. Barratt said. "But I wanted to introduce you to Mr. Jimmy Park, who will be putting to use the results you gentlemen produce."

The three nodded cursorily in the direction of Jimmy.

He wasn't what was on their minds.

"Yes, Mr. Barratt," said one of the three. "We're *working* at producing results for you, sir."

"But it's not coming easily," said another.

"We think it's some kind of substitution code," said the third. "Perhaps book based. But without the key it's difficult indeed. Number codes come so much simpler!"

The young man's two comrades nodded in agreement.

Mr. Barratt ignored the trio's extenuation. Instead, he turned to Jimmy. "These three gentlemen..." He indicated them singly. "William, Robert, and David, come to us from Cal Tech, where Albert Einstein taught for a few years. They are surely the best and brightest, and they have patriotically agreed to settle this difficult problem for us. And to do so *quickly* and without excuses of any kind because it is of the utmost importance. Isn't that a fine thing, Mr. Park?"

Jimmy nodded, though he knew the message wasn't really directed at him.

The problem was this:

While Mr. Barratt's organization held a high degree of confidence that the three murders of the night before had been intended, not as warnings to Jimmy Park but as a single, encrypted invitation for Jimmy to join the Orchid's nefarious organization, they had been unable to discern from the clues how Jimmy was to make contact with the Jap spy ring. Hence, the code breakers from Cal Tech. One life-sized photograph of each of the three blood-scrawled Japanese messages hung beside each of the three chalkboards.

"First, we brought in experts in Japanese calligraphy, which is far more complicated than I ever imagined, to examine the photographs," Mr. Barratt explained. "They discerned that the order in which the strokes were made for each Japanese character was unconventional, even inaccurate." He indicated the characters. "They may look like chicken scratches to me, but there's method to them. It turns out that when forming any word you don't just make the marks but you make them *in a proscribed order.*"

Naturally, Jimmy already knew this (being fluent in both spoken and written Japanese). But he nodded as if it were news.

Mr. Barratt continued, "So, our Japanese experts isolated the strokes that had been made out of order. Laying these strokes atop one another, our linguists managed to construct a single coherent character that, at first, we thought might be the secret message."

"And?" Jimmy pressed.

Mr. Barratt sighed. "The character was the word for 'horse's ass.'"

Unamused, Jimmy snapped angrily, "So this whole thing is a mere taunt?"

Mr. Barratt shook his head. "We still believe there's a real message hidden in there. One intended for you. So we're working from their English translations."

The messages were scrawled in chalk, one on each of the blackboards:

> "And so it begins for you, white devils."
> "We are watching your eyes, even as they fail to see us."
> "Accept your friend's life as a personal gift."

The coin-rattling code breaker stepped toward Jimmy to explain. "Naturally, in accordance with Occam's Razor, we began with the simplest possibilities, simply scrambling the words in every possible order, coming up with a few interesting modernist poems along the way but nothing remotely suggestive of how you were to make contact with the Jap organization."

"Next, we took the translated messages apart letter-by-letter," said the chin-scratching code-breaker. "This entailed considerably more work, as the possibilities significantly increased, requiring our best efforts. Again, we concocted numerous alternate messages, but none seems directive."

"Have you made a list of these messages?" Mr. Barratt asked.

"Yes, it's almost a hundred pages, typed single-spaced."

"That doesn't seem so much, since we know what we're looking for," Mr. Barratt observed.

"Do we?" the third code-breaker asked.

Mr. Barratt opened his palms in frustration. "A secret location of some kind. Is that so difficult?"

He waited, but none of the code breakers dared answer.

"Boys, your failing here is not an option," Mr. Barratt said, calmly.

"Well, it may not be so simple as just scrambling or unscrambling letters," the head-scratcher said.

"See, if it's a book replacement code cleverly disguised to look like three discreet and circumstantially appropriate messages, then we're in trouble, as we'll require the key if we're *ever* going to break it," continued the coin-jiggler, daring to meet Mr. Barratt's gaze. "Desire alone will not be enough, sir. Even veiled threats won't work."

"I'm not threatening you, boys," Mr. Barratt said, threateningly.

The head scratching code-breaker looked at Jimmy. "Do you know what a book replacement code is?"

Jimmy nodded.

Among multiple variations, the most common book replacement code used particular pages from a particular edition of a book to act as the key to encoded messages. For example, if pages 265–290 of the first edition of *The Sun Also Rises* were the key, then the first letter of the coded message would correspond to that letter's first use on page 265, thereby revealing a word in the Hemingway text that was also the first word of the *de-coded* message. Subsequent letters in the coded message would refer to progressive instances in the book, indicating corresponding, de-coded words. To make such a code work also as coherent statements, such as the bloody threats written now on the blackboard, required true mastery. But without the key (the particular book and pages), there was no viable way to decode the secret message.

"Do any particular books come to mind, Jimmy?" Mr. Barratt asked.

Jimmy considered. He shook his head.

"Maybe books aren't his thing," one of the code-breakers said.

"Don't underestimate Jimmy," Mr. Barratt snapped in response. "He's an experienced operative."

The three code-breakers turned from Mr. Barratt to Jimmy, giving him the once over, focusing with obvious disapproval on his sporty suit and fashionable Florsheims.

"Sometimes, experience alone won't do it," one said.

"A little more Sherlock Holmes, a little less Sam Spade," another added.

Jimmy smiled. "Give me a piece of chalk, boys."

They handed one over.

Jimmy walked to the first chalkboard. He studied it. "You know, when I was playing baseball for my high school team in Glendale I used to steal the catcher's signs whenever I reached second base," he said without turning around. "Then I'd relay the upcoming pitch to our batter and he'd invariably knock me in. But there was one team in our league whose catcher used signs I couldn't ever steal." He remained facing the chalkboard as he continued. "How complicated *were* his signs, I wondered, frustrated. Until, that is, I realized his signs were not complicated at all. They'd been tricky to me only because they held no shred of trickery, except in my own mind. From that time forward, we never lost to that team again."

"Too bad we're not playing baseball," one of the code-breakers commented.

Jimmy said nothing but wrote the word, "Pike" above the quote that read, "And so it begins for you, white devils."

He moved to the second chalkboard and wrote the word, "Gypsy" above the quote that read, "We are watching your eyes, even as they fail to see us."

At the third chalkboard he wrote, "Fortuna" above the words "Accept your friend's life as a personal gift."

"The victims," Mr. Barratt observed.

Jimmy turned. "The messages in blood mean nothing. They were merely intended to tie the crimes together and maybe to give a little poke with that 'horse's ass' business. And their translations are equally useless. All that really matters is the names of the victims."

"Pike . . ."

"Gypsy . . ."

"Fortuna . . ." muttered the three code-breakers.

"Isn't it obvious?" Jimmy inquired.

Mr. Barratt broke into a wide grin. He had it.

"A Gypsy fortune-teller named Pike?" one of the code-breakers ventured.

"Almost," Jimmy said. "Have any of you heard of 'The Pike,' an amusement park in Long Beach?"

"With the big roller coaster?" asked another of the code-breakers.

Jimmy nodded. "The Gypsy fortune-teller *at* the Pike."

The three young men from Cal Tech threw their arms open. "How could we have missed it?"

"Because it was too simple," Jimmy said, humbly. "You boys are purebred racing greyhounds and I'm just a dog with a nose for the obvious."

They looked at him with new respect.

"So the three victims died just because, together, their names constituted this message," Mr. Barratt mused.

"Nobody said we were going up against choirboys," Jimmy reminded his spy handler.

"I think you're going to do all right," Mr. Barratt said.

"Thanks," Jimmy answered, though he knew this was just the beginning.

Mr. Barratt picked up a telephone in the corner of the room. "Get me a secure line with all the men who were in my office this past hour." He paused, listening to the voice at the other end. "No, I don't want you to call me back, I'll hold," he snapped. "I need that call now!"

Jimmy and the code breakers remained silent as Mr. Barratt waited to be put through.

After a moment, Mr. Barratt turned and whispered to Jimmy, his protégé, "I guess we can call off some of our dogs in Jap town."

Jimmy nodded, though he didn't know about any specific agents working for Barratt in Jap Town.

Still holding, the spy-handler turned and spoke loudly enough for the cryptologists from Cal Tech to hear too. "It's funny, boys, but we thought for a while that a wretched old fortune-teller on Alameda, a real crone, whose place we searched and roughed up a bit, might be involved with the Orchid's syndicate. A Jap instead of a Gypsy, but still . . . *fortune-teller*, what a coincidence!" He adjusted the receiver against his ear. "Then again, we've also been doing surveillance on a Jap Town dentist named Shinoda and some doctors' offices too. So there goes the coincidence. I guess you just file it all under the category of 'leaving no stone unturned.' In any case, Jimmy's breakthrough here today changes everything!" Suddenly, he returned his attention to the phone. After a moment of listening, he shouted into the receiver: "I don't care if the senator is in transit! Tell them to pull the darned train over, if necessary!"

❧

Excerpt from a letter dated November 22, 1942:

. . . lovely, but I think you can do better, even if the fortune-teller in Little Tokyo is <u>real</u>. Don't get me wrong. I appreciate and value the details of the actual down-town LA that you pepper throughout your book. Further, that you've personally visited this old soothsayer lends verisi-militude to the scene; however, it comes as no great surprise to the reader if the Orchid's nefarious organization proves to be headquartered in Little Tokyo. For that reason, I suggest you choose another loca-tion for the evil soothsayer—something unex-pected and rich with dramatic possibility. Perhaps an amusement park. (We have Coney Island here in New York; what is the Los Angeles equivalent?) And perhaps the for-tune-teller should be a Gypsy rather than Japanese, adding a layer between your hero and the Orchid herself. Of course, I under-stand that this will require your going back to revise the "clues" contained in the three murders. But the name "Fortuna" still works. So you really only have to figure out two new names that serve as clues.

Look, this soothsayer business ulti-

mately leads to the climactic confrontation, and so why not set it in a more
chaotic place? Crowds, roller coaster, calliope, house of mirrors . . . Indulge. Just
give us excitement! And the unexpected!
These are the hallmarks of a good thriller.
As for your portrayal of the actual Japanese soothsayer in Little Tokyo . . . it's
quite evocative, but I suggest you save it
for your memoirs of life in LA before the
war or some such thing.

I love the little, real touches, but
don't ever let reality limit you!

Warmest,

Maxine Wakefield
Maxine Wakefield,
Associate Editor,
Metropolitan Modern Mysteries, Inc.

P.S. I've enclosed with this letter my blue-
penciled revisions to your proposed "bio"
of the pseudonymous William Thorne. You'll
see that I've made some changes and addi-
tions, as I think we were a bit cautious or
conservative in some of our original con-
cepts. This is, after all, for distribu-
tion by the publicity department. So why
not allow your reader to be nearly as fascinated by the author Thorne as he/she is
by your fictional characters? Aren't we justified in bending a few publishing rules
in light of the unusual and unfair commercial problems that your real name poses
these days? So I've retained your idea that
due to his sensitive police/government work

Thorne is not the author's real name (you're right that we don't want anybody thinking they can look him up for a magazine profile etc.) But rather than describing him as a mere veteran of the Great War I've made him a Congressional Medal of Honor winner. Why not? If a journalist should attempt to contact actual honorees to determine the "real" identity of the author, the reporter will, naturally, be met only by denials. And yet isn't that exactly what the "real" William Thorne would do? Deny. Isn't this fun, Takumi! Also, rather than being a mere LAPD detective, I've made Thorne a Fed with a distinguished history of bringing to justice Yakuza gangsters who, for decades, have attempted to infiltrate and corrupt American cities by distributing heroin and other illicit substances to our youth. Now a "consultant" with the LAPD, Thorne has written the novel not strictly for literary purposes but to warn the American public about the real threat of Fifth Column activities in our own communities. Oh, and I made him a father of four, married to his high school sweetheart for almost two decades. If you think that's putting it on a little thick, let me know. We don't want to get called out for our little publishing misdemeanor.

THE REVISED—CHAPTER SIX

Write the characters in dust . . .

—Sir Walter Scott

Sumida watched Czernicek approach the square from the direction of the diner, a toothpick angled in his mouth. The big detective walked like he owned the city, even though he seemed to be as mysteriously cut off from its inhabitants as Sumida. Drawing near, he tossed his toothpick into some bushes. He didn't sit on the bench but loomed over Sumida. His voice was full of derision. "So now I suggest you get your ass off this bench and go back to the periodicals room to catch up on the events of the last couple months. It's information. Maybe you'll find something in it. That's what detectives do, Sumida. *Real* detectives. Actually, I'd have thought the same was true of college instructors, like you, but who knows how your type operates? What kind of teacher were you anyway? I've forgotten."

"Oriental art history," Sumida answered.

"Figures . . . that's a limp dick subject."

"So what's your list of virile subjects, Mr. Academia?"

Czernicek shrugged. "Law. Medicine. Engineering. But you'd be no good at any of those things."

For a time in his late teens, Sumida had studied engineering. But he wasn't going to defend himself, wasn't going to engage Czernicek in his asinine assertions.

"Oh, you people are good at some things," Czernicek continued, burying his hands in his coat pocket. "I'll give you that. Good gardeners, for example. And I've seen plenty of small-time fishermen down in San Pedro who seemed to know what they were doing. Even a little modest farming in Paramount and down in Orange County. Oh, and cut-rate dentistry over in Jap town. Damn near pain-free. I gave up Caucasian dentists long ago. I think it's your people's squinty eyes and little hands. And your older women make good crafts, like the ladies that turn sheets of paper into swans or grasshoppers. And your younger women . . . well, do you want me to elaborate on their most outstanding attributes?"

"That's enough, Czernicek," Sumida answered.

Czernicek laughed. "I'm just trying to be honest and companionable."

"You're an asshole."

"Yeah. Anyway, meet me tonight at my hotel," Czernicek said, turning away.

Sumida watched him stride across the plaza, eventually disappearing into a crowd.

Only then did Sumida gather himself up.

He wasn't going back to the periodicals room. He already knew that the catastrophe at Pearl Harbor had changed the world for millions (including every Nisei, like himself, trying to peaceably make his or her way in this city and, doubtless, in every city on the West Coast). And he already knew that there had been no report of Kyoko's murder in the edition of the *LA Times* where, the previous year, there had been a two-column story with a picture.

He had another plan.

Sumida knew of a woman in Little Tokyo who practiced traditional forms of fortune-telling. Being an academic, he'd never put much faith in such practices. And he surely knew better than to mention such a thing to Czernicek. But the last hours had demonstrated that perhaps Shakespeare had gotten it right when he wrote that there were more things in heaven and earth than were dreamt of in your philosophy. If a skilled old woman could discern the future by reading the cracks on a heated tortoise shell (*kiboku*), or interpreting the cries of passing birds (*toriura*), or the words of passersby (*tsujiura*), or by the tossing and reading of a large number of bamboo sticks called *zeichiku*, then might she also be able to discern some explanation for Sam's predicament? Anything at all would put him ahead of where he stood now, which was nowhere.

The ten bucks ought to do the trick.

The challenge, however, would be returning to that neighborhood. Since Kyoko's death, he had set foot there only when his investigation had required it. For example, he'd interviewed her former employer, Dr. Shinoda, and talked with all of her working acquaintances—none of whom had even been contacted in the LAPD's initial, farcical investigation. But it had come to nothing. And each time Sumida had entered the sixteen square blocks that constituted Little Tokyo, he suffered the weight of Kyoko's loss all over again. It was not only her place of work, it had been their place for fun. Early in their marriage, they'd dined at her favorite hole-in-the-wall restaurant near Temple and Alameda and window-shopped and drank sake and joked in a playful mix of English and Japanese with other Nisei. So now no place was more painful for him. Her presence remained everywhere he looked in the neighborhood.

He knew he would still feel her there.

Yet he suspected that when he spoke her name in Shinoda's dental office he'd be met only with empty expressions. As if she'd never been. Still, he had to try. And if his questions came to nothing, then he'd continue on to the fortune-teller, who might tell him what he was (a figment of his own imagination?), or why he was here, or, at least, how he was supposed to find a way to keep going.

❧

Excerpt from chapter nine of *The Orchid and the Secret Agent*, a novel by William Thorne
     Metropolitan Modern Mysteries, Inc., New York, N.Y., 1945

... At a quarter to five, Jimmy Park and his good friend Joe Lucas settled into an isolated booth at the far end of the Parkside Diner, across the street from Pershing Square. Since the outbreak of war, the square had ceased to be lit in the evenings, and so now, as dusk approached outside the big picture window, the square appeared as a large garden of shadows. Soon, the diner would draw its blackout curtains, eliminating the view of the square altogether.

"Get the chicken pot pie," Jimmy suggested.

"It's a little early for dinner, don't you think, Jimmy?"

Jimmy shrugged an apology. "I wanted to see you, Joe. And the rest of my night is pretty booked up."

"Oh, excuse me, Mr. Cole Porter. Thanks for fitting me into your busy social schedule."

Jimmy sighed. "There'll be no social engagements for me tonight."

Joe looked at his friend. After a moment, he acquiesced, making a show of picking up his menu. "You disappear for the whole day," he said, scanning the daily special on the handwritten index card paper-clipped to the top of the menu. "You leave *me* to clean up that bloody mess at your place, which, incidentally, has been put down both in the papers and in the DA's office as an accidental death, and now you want to *tell me what to eat*?"

"Sorry," Jimmy answered.

"Sorry for what, the mess you left me with or your dinner recommendation?" Joe pressed.

"I make no apologies for the chicken pot pie," Jimmy said, smiling sheepishly.

But Joe was in no laughing mood. "And when I say 'cleaning up,' I don't just mean the blood, you understand?" He took a sip from his water glass, his hand shaking just perceptibly.

"I appreciate your getting that wall painted so quick and carting off that sofa," Jimmy said. "That's going above and beyond the call of duty, buddy."

Joe shook his head. "I didn't pick up any paint brush. My nephew Tommy painted over the Jap scribbles, *after* the police photographers were done with it." He stopped and swallowed hard.

Jimmy waited, letting his friend say what he needed to say.

"Oh don't worry, I did my part," Joe continued, shaking his head in disgust. "Look, I played it exactly like your FBI guys asked me. You

don't have to worry about that. I understand things are real complicated these days. The department understands that too. But hell, I'm
your friend. It's time you told me what was going on here. And who
took my .38 Special?"

Jimmy shrugged. "You know there are some things I'm not at
liberty to say."

Joe nodded. But that didn't mean he wasn't going to give his friend
a hard time. "Well, don't think that paint job was a gift. You'll be getting
a bill from my nephew any day now."

"Good."

"And he don't work cheap."

"I would hope not," Jimmy said.

"And *I* didn't cart off the goddamn blood-soaked sofa," Joe continued. "The Feds took it this morning."

"That makes sense," Jimmy said.

"Yeah, well . . . at least something makes sense."

Jimmy said nothing.

Joe looked down at the table. "The worst part of it was my being
asked to lie to that poor woman across the street about her husband
having 'fallen down and hit his head.'"

"Funny thing is . . ." Jimmy started. "The coroner said he *did* have
a lump on the back of his head, suggesting he'd been knocked unconscious, but was still alive, when they slit his throat."

"Is that supposed to make me feel better?"

Jimmy looked away, sympathetically. He lowered his voice,
though no one was seated near them. "There are some things that
can't be allowed to get out to the public. Like what became of poor
Tony Fortuna. The carnage. And the Jap writing in blood on the wall.
You know as well as I do it'd panic people to know how truly evil our
enemies are. And, worse, how nearby."

"What did the Jap writing say?"

Jimmy shook his head.

"But you told the widow the truth? She's in on it?"

"No. That would have only endangered her." Jimmy stopped.

Joe sighed. "Okay, national security. . . . But does that mean that Fortuna's widow isn't going to get to see her husband's body?"

"That slash across his throat would blow the 'accident' angle, right?"

"Yeah," Joe said, distractedly rubbing the side of his face with one hand. "But it don't seem right."

"I agree, Joe. It's *not* right. But it's necessary."

"So what'll our people do?" Joe pressed. "About the funeral?"

Jimmy tapped his fingers on the Formica tabletop. After a moment, he answered flatly, "There's going to be a 'mix-up' at the mortuary. Sadly, her husband's body 'inadvertently' will be cremated."

Joe's jaw dropped. "Like some kind of Hindu?"

Jimmy looked away.

"Poor woman," Joe said.

"I agree," Jimmy answered. He turned and looked out the window, but now he saw more of his own reflection than the shadowy square. Nonetheless, he didn't turn back to Joe. "These weren't my decisions. They were made at the highest levels. And the stakes . . . well, they're even higher." He looked at Joe. "You trust me?"

After a moment, in answer, Joe tapped his fist twice on the tabletop and nodded.

"Good," Jimmy said.

"So why'd you pick this place for us to meet?" Joe asked.

"It's a clean, well-lighted place."

Joe recognized the phrase. "That's a Hemingway story," he observed.

Jimmy nodded.

"A story about death," Joe added.

Jimmy didn't want to talk about that. "I just wanted a public place," he said.

"Why?"

"Safe."

"From who?"

Jimmy decided to give his friend more than he'd originally intended. "That's what my job is now. To find out."

"What have you got yourself involved with?" Joe asked, his deep concern manifesting as lines on his forehead.

Jimmy chuckled as if it were nothing.

Joe looked Jimmy in the eye. "Wait a minute . . ." The wheels of his mind were turning. "It's not the FBI you're working for. And it's not Army or Navy Intelligence either. It's some other kind of organization that calls the shots for all the others. Some government group that I don't even know the name of."

Jimmy wasn't going to lie to his friend. "The group doesn't really even have any name, yet."

Joe sat back in the Naugahyde booth. "Yeah, that's how you get away with covering up murder," Joe said, a note of bitterness slipping into his voice.

Jimmy understood. Joe Lucas was a good cop. He only wanted the best. "Look Joe, we're going to get the killers. That's the whole idea."

Just then, the waitress, a good-looking kid in a mustard-stained uniform, arrived at their booth. She looked at Jimmy. "Sorry, but we don't serve Japs anymore."

Jimmy started to give his usual answer, but Joe stopped him with a wave of his hand.

"Look, I'm LAPD and this man's name is Jimmy Park." Joe spoke with the brusque manner of a motorcycle cop giving a speeding ticket. "And he's of *Korean* ancestry."

She looked doubtful. "What's with cops bringing Orientals into my station today?"

They didn't follow.

Joe removed his badge from his suit jacket pocket and showed it to her. "You can trust me."

"Oh, well, that's OK then." She removed her order pad from a large, hip pocket on her uniform and a pencil from within her nest of blonde hair. "What can I get for you and your Korean friend, Officer?"

"Chicken pot pies for the both of us," Joe said, folding his menu and handing it up to the girl.

The girl turned and started away.

When she was out of earshot, Joe turned to Jimmy. "So, can I help this no-name organization?"

Jimmy looked at Joe. "There may come a time that we need a friend on the inside of the LAPD, but that's not what I wanted to talk to you about tonight."

"Oh, I see. You wanted to talk baseball," Joe snapped, sarcastically.

Jimmy reached inside his suit coat pocket and removed a sheaf of five handwritten pages, folded vertically. He dropped it on the tabletop between them.

Joe picked it up. "What is it?"

"My last will and testament," Jimmy answered.

Joe said nothing.

"You're in it," Jimmy said, brightly.

Joe didn't smile back. "Why do you need to give this to me now?"

Jimmy didn't hesitate. "You know why, Joe."

"Does Sun know about this?"

Jimmy shook his head. He knew his girlfriend would take it hard. "She'd just worry."

Joe nodded. He picked up the folded sheets and slipped them into his own jacket pocket.

For a moment the men were silent.

"This chicken pot pie better be as good as you say," Joe said at last, slapping his hand down on the table.

Jimmy shrugged. "How would I know? I've never had it!"

❧

Excerpt from a letter dated December 19, 1942:

```
      . . . more balls to keep up in the air than
      any juggler would dare attempt. But that's
      the nature of the novelist's task. With that
      in mind, it occurs to me that, while your
      original,    discarded   submission   (Sumida,
```

Czernicek, etc.) had plenty of sexual moti-
vations, including the murder, this revision has very little. Of course, the nature
of the new book, being a novel of espionage,
somewhat excuses this, exchanging international stakes for personal ones; also, we're
going to meet the Orchid soon enough and she
will bring tremendous *femme fatale* power.
But in your latest submission to me, with
Jimmy and Joe in the diner, I found myself
both delighted by the complexity and warmth
of the men's friendship and also a little
worried. I'm sure you'd agree that the last
thing we want is for readers to suspect that
there is any queer aspect to the Jimmy/Joe
relationship. Yet in your manuscript there
have been, as yet, <u>no</u> mentions of women by
either man. As we've been crackling along
at an excellent action pace, I understand
that there's been little attention paid to
Jimmy's personal life at all. However, I'm
wondering if you can include some sort of
brief reference to Jimmy's having a girlfriend in this scene to assuage any suspicions your readers may develop regarding
this otherwise quite moving moment of male
bonding. (Please understand that here in
New York I have more than one discreet homo-
sexual friend and that I hold a live-and-
let-live attitude in my personal life, <u>but</u>
remember you are writing for a general and
very broad readership.) Besides, I'm sure the
idea of Jimmy and Joe's closeness as being
anything but good, old-fashioned friendship
has never even occurred to you. That's what
you need a jaded New York editor for, right?
So, even a slight reference in this scene to

a girlfriend will do in your revision. And
perhaps a reference in an earlier chapter
(back at Jimmy's house?) about Jimmy's girlfriend and maybe Joe having a wife, too.

Sincerely,

Maxine Wakefield
Maxine Wakefield,
Associate Editor,
Metropolitan Modern Mysteries, Inc.

THE REVISED—CHAPTER SIX cont'd.

By the time Sumida had trekked across downtown, avoiding any groups
of men he saw coming along the sidewalk in his direction, the last rays of
the winter sun cast shadows about the Little Tokyo streets, which were
uncharacteristically empty of pedestrian traffic. Many of the shops that
ordinarily stayed open late were already closed. Almost all displayed in
their plate glass windows either American flags or signs that read "WE
ARE AMERICANS." A few windows had been boarded up, shards of
their shattered glass swept from the sidewalk into the gutter, and a five-
and-ten-cent store in the middle of a block of brick storefronts had been
burned out. The cigar stands and little candy shops were gone. Things
had changed. Still, Sumida felt the old ache in the pit of his stomach
when he ventured onto these streets, where he'd shared happy hours
with Kyoko. Of course, he knew that global events—war—dwarfed his
loss. But that knowledge didn't diminish the ache he felt for his wife. It
only added a sense of selfish shame to it.

Dr. Shinoda's dental office waiting room was empty when Sumida
walked in. On the walls hung three framed WPA posters of National
Parks. Sumida, art historian, considered the posters a cut above the

ordinary treacly waiting room fare. And very American too, which was doubtless a benefit in these fragile times. The big coffee table, centered between a worn sofa and a pair of velveteen end chairs, held issues of the *Saturday Evening Post, Time, Life, Look, National Geographic,* and a handful of Japanese-language magazines, some dating as far back as the mid-thirties. Atop the magazines were scattered refolded sections of that morning's *LA Times.*

The newspaper stopped him.

He was struck by what his uncle would describe as *seiten no heki-reki,* an idea as abrupt as a thunderclap out of the sky.

Earlier in the periodicals room of the library . . .

When he'd asked for the *LA Times* edition that he presumed (mistakenly) would contain the article about his wife's murder . . .

It had been checked out earlier that day . . . by Czernicek.

Why?

Sumida swallowed hard. The date had to mean something to Czernicek, just as it did to Sumida. Could the cop have been looking for some *other* article in that particular edition? Very unlikely. Might his have been a lingering professional interest in Kyoko's case? No. During the investigation, Czernicek had worn his disinterest like a medal of honor. Indeed, he'd been more an active impediment than a merely disinterested party.

So might he have had a personal interest in Kyoko's murder that Sumida had never considered?

"May I help you, sir?"

Sumida turned, startled out of his reverie, and refocused his attention on an unfamiliar, middle-aged woman who sat at the receptionist's desk behind the open, sliding-glass window, where Kyoko used to sit.

"I'm afraid we're booked for today," she continued. "But I can make an appointment for you later in the week."

"Is this still Dr. Shinoda's office?"

She nodded. "God willing, we'll get to stay."

"In business?"

"In our homes," she answered, as if it should be obvious.

Sumida had overheard talk coming from the counter of the Parkview

Diner that the government was considering relocating all West Coast Japanese Americans to detention camps, a prospect unthinkable as recently as this past December sixth. (Or was it just last night?)

"Do you know a woman named Kyoko Sumida?" he asked.

The receptionist considered. "That name's not familiar to me."

"She used to hold your same job for Dr. Shinoda," Sumida continued. "Then she was promoted to office manager."

The woman shook her head. "That's not possible. I've been with Dr. Shinoda since he opened his practice. And I'm the office manager."

Sumida understood the futility of arguing these points. "I see."

"So, do you need an appointment?" she asked.

"No." He turned to go and then stopped. Hadn't Czernicek said something about being a patient of a Japanese dentist? Yes, this was what detectives did. "On second thought, I would like an appointment," he said, turning back to the receptionist. "Just a checkup and teeth cleaning."

She flipped open a large appointment book. "We have ten a.m. available next Monday," she said.

"That'll do just fine."

"Your name?"

"Henry Czernicek," he said.

She looked up at him, confused. "What?"

"Just write it on an appointment card, please." He patted the counter casually. "My name and the date and time of my appointment."

She still looked confused. "But . . ."

Sumida explained away the name. "My father was a white man," he lied.

"That's not what's confusing me," she said. "It's . . . how do you spell that last name?"

"Oh, right," Sumida said. He did his best with the spelling.

She gave him a card.

He slipped it into his suit jacket.

❧

Excerpt from chapter ten of *The Orchid and the Secret Agent*, a novel by
William Thorne
      Metropolitan Modern Mysteries, Inc., New York, N.Y., 1945

… A group of frat boys posing a serious threat to Jimmy's safety as he
cut through the alley behind the Parkside Diner on his way back to the
parking lot? This was the last thing Jimmy thought he'd have to worry
about just now, particularly in light of the more obvious threat posed by the
murderous Japanese spy ring, which he was just hours from attempting to
infiltrate. He hadn't time for this nonsense. And the USA could not afford
his being delayed by stupidity. But there they were … six college men in
lettermen's jackets, at least four of them big enough to be football linemen,
all of them red-faced and belligerent from too much alcohol, three of them
armed with tire irons, the other three brandishing hammers.

      "Damned Jap," the burliest muttered, balling his free hand into a
fist. "What makes you think you can just walk around after dark?"

      The others laughed.

      "I'm not a Jap," Jimmy said. "My name's Park. Korean. Now let me pass."

      "Ha!" the talkative frat boy belched. "That's what they all say!"

      Jimmy was confident he could take the frat boys, even with their tire
irons and hammers. But six was a lot. Sure, he'd ultimately leave them
scattered and unconscious in the alley, but not before suffering damage
himself. … Maybe broken ribs, nose, teeth, jaw, or even a broken hand
from fending off their weapons. The best he could hope for would be
bruises and lumps. While a little ice and a few shots of rye would make
such injuries better, he still didn't want to show up black-eyed in Long
Beach to see the Gypsy fortune-teller, looking like he'd been coerced by
the Feds into taking the Jap spy ring's blood-soaked bait. No, he needed
to look his best tonight. He needed the spy ring to *want* him on their
side. And who'd want to recruit a human punching bag?

      Unfortunately, Joe had cut across Pershing Square after they'd
parted at the diner and so Jimmy couldn't call for his buddy's help.
Nonetheless, he glanced back in the direction from which he'd come.
In the dusk, a small crowd of curious pedestrians had gathered at the

end of the alley, effectively blocking it. He turned. A small crowd was gathering at the other end too.

Jimmy called to them. "Hey, somebody want to talk some sense to these young men?"

None of the spectators moved.

What they seemed to want was to see a beating.

"Look, I have ID," Jimmy said, turning back to the boys.

The frat boys moved forward.

"We don't trust your kind, whatever false documents you may have," said one.

If Jimmy were to take out his .45 and fire off a few warning shots—the obvious answer—he'd scatter the cowardly collegians but he'd also create a panic among the spectators, likely resulting in police involvement, delay, and possibly even newspaper or radio coverage, which might discourage the Jap spy ring from their recruitment of him even more than a few broken bones and a black eye. So he decided to just take out all six collegians with his hands and feet. Sure, there might be a few lumps to endure—but what else could he do?

He moved forward, reminding himself that these collegians were little more than drunken fools. They'd earned a beating . . . but no more than that. He'd use his Taekwondo skills to break no bones, with the exception of a few noses or jaws. These were Americans of military age, and soon they'd be serving the United States in the war. Naturally, a small part of Jimmy would have relished using his hands and feet to silence their unwarranted aggression by putting them all in the intensive care unit. He was only human. But he'd go easy on the boys, leaving them merely bruised and concussed outpatients who could be stitched up in the emergency room.

"Look, he's coming toward us!" one of the collegians said, disbelieving.

"That's right, boys," Jimmy said, calmly.

He took care of business, wading through the bruisers with flashing hands and footwork, using their own hammers and tire irons against them, leaving them scattered and bloodied and unconscious. They hardly laid a hand on him.

The spectators at either end of the alley were stunned; after a moment, a few of the beefier men began to cautiously move forward. This could get even uglier, Jimmy thought. Meanwhile, other spectators scattered, likely to alert the police.

Jimmy needed to get gone.

Hemmed in now on both sides of the alley, he jumped lithely onto a garbage can and reached up to a window casing, pulling himself up to a brick outcropping. From there, he leapfrogged to the next outcropping and the next and the next, until he had scaled the sheer side of the building and hopped over the ledge onto the roof.

He looked down at the alley.

The spectators gazed up at him with their mouths agape, as if he were some kind of comic book character.

But he knew the truth about himself. He was just a United States government operative who was pretty darn good at his job.

He waved down to the startled spectators and started across the rooftop, leaping an alley to another building and then another and another, and in this way he made his escape.

꙳

Excerpt from a letter dated January 30, 1943:

. . . very effective to demonstrate that Jimmy is not only an enthusiastic agent for America but also an extraordinarily capable one. However, my trusty blue pencil has cut some of the most offensive dialogue that you gave to the drunken college boys. Don't misunderstand: I support your wanting to depict the broad racism currently in America's streets. That's admirable. But describing the college boys' verbal antipathy toward Mexicans and Negroes, in addition to "Japs," goes too

far for our purposes. I know from the note
you included with the chapter that you feel
adamant about changing little or nothing in
this scene. But, quite honestly, even <u>after</u>
my cleaning it up (which you'll see on the
extensively marked typescript, included
with this letter), it still strains the
limits of the genre and the war department's
sensibilities. Besides, most of our readers
are white men who may have gotten stupidly
drunk once or twice and said things that
they may later have regretted. Who do you
want to alienate? In this light, I've indicated places where you can show just how
broad-minded Jimmy is by his considering
the eventual usefulness of these youths to
the coming war effort for the USA.

Look, I believe we get away with the
scene at all because, as ugly as the white
boys' racism and threats of violence are,
the flip side of the circumstance is that
those same ugly elements serve as secondary
justification for the internment of Japanese
Americans (which, sadly, you are only too
familiar with); that is, Japanese Americans
have been relocated to camps, in part, <u>for
their own safety</u>. In that light, how then
can the censors at the war office object to
what you've written when the specific depic-
tion of racism toward Japanese serves to
justify as humanitarian the government's
recent actions all up and down the West
Coast? You understand that <u>I</u> do not favor
the internment, but I am merely speaking as
your partner in making every scene in your
book viable within the restrictions of the
genre and our complex times. Do you see

that I take all your ambitions seriously?
Do you know that I consider your book more
than a mere spy thriller? Don't you appreciate that I share your mixed feelings
about a story that derives drama from the
internal threat of Japanese infiltration in
our West Coast cities, even as you, a talented and law-abiding Nisei, are interned?
What a brave man you are!

I know your novel as it exists today
isn't what you originally planned. But
isn't it quite good anyway? Besides, circumstances change. We've all been affected
by the war. On a personal note, my husband
was reported missing-in-action last week on
Guadalcanal. I believe in my heart he will
turn up any day, perhaps wounded but generally sound. I have to believe it; otherwise
I'd lose my mind. I ought not to have told
you this. . . . It is really quite unpro-
fessional. But I feel we are growing close
in this creative process, you in Manzanar,
me in Manhattan. I do hope that, despite
what you described in your note as your
"unyielding commitment to the dialogue as
it is," you can see fit to allow my cuts for
all the reasons I've outlined above. Otherwise, I see no sense continuing with this
project, as neither our readership nor the
war department will endorse a scene that
makes generalized racists of the very young
men who, for all their faults, will soon
be on foreign shores in the uniform of the
United States.

Please let me know if you can live with
my revisions.

Your humble and hopeful friend,

Maxine Wakefield

Maxine Wakefield,

Associate Editor,

Metropolitan Modern Mysteries, Inc.

❦

THE REVISED—CHAPTER SIX cont'd.

Exiting Dr. Shinoda's office, Sumida found that the handful of stores and restaurants that remained open in Little Tokyo were nonetheless as dark behind their newly mandated black-out curtains as the shuttered businesses. Sumida knew that the small storefront of the fortune-teller never closed, as she lived in an apartment upstairs and did not keep regular hours. Kyoko had visited her at least a dozen times, claiming that the fortune-teller served more as a kind of psychological counselor than as a clairvoyant. But Sam knew his wife took much of what the old woman said as irrefutable, supernaturally acquired truth. He had accompanied Kyoko on a few of her trips here but always made a point of waiting outside, allowing no crack in the armor of his rationality. Now, with rational explanations elusive, he wondered if Kyoko might have had it right all along. (Though of what use was a soothsayer if she failed to warn a woman of impending murder?)

The fortune-teller's storefront was as still as most of the others. It took Sumida a moment to notice that both the English letters and the Japanese characters for "fortune-teller," 占い師, along with the old woman's name (which eluded him just now) had been scratched off the big, black plate-glass window, which had never allowed passersby to catch a glimpse of the inside. He hoped the soothsayer was still there. Near the mail slot, he found the button and pressed.

He heard a buzzing sound.

Nothing, so he pressed again.

After a moment, a second-floor window slid up and open directly above him. The old woman's head poked out, straining around the heavy curtains. She looked down at Sumida's upturned face, the tendons in her wrinkled neck stretched taut. Sumida thought of a turtle, which seemed apt, since one of her soothsaying techniques involved the use of a tortoise shell.

He called up to her respectfully by her title, fortune-teller: "*Uranaishi-san*, I need your services."

She held his gaze for a moment, then looked right and left, surveying the dark street, which was deserted but for another old woman a few doors down who sat on her front steps shelling beans. The streetlamps remained off. A few cars passed, their headlights reduced to mere slits.

"The white people do not allow my business anymore," she said. Her English was good, but accented. "Too Japanese. Pagan. No trouble, please. Sorry."

"Wait!" he called up, before she could pull her head back inside. "My wife used to come to see you." He held up the sawbuck. "I can pay you ten dollars."

She looked at the bill as he waved it.

"You make trouble for me?" she asked.

"No, *Uranaishi-san*."

She pulled her head inside and a minute or two later the front door locks turned. The door opened a crack. One of the old woman's cataract-fogged eyes peeked through the gap. "No trouble for me?" she asked again.

"That's right."

"The police cause trouble."

"I'm not with the police," he said to her in Japanese.

Her exposed eye moved up and down, taking him in. "No, I guess you wouldn't be," she answered in English. She stepped back, opening the door just wide enough for him to slip in after her.

Then she closed and locked the door behind him.

Inside, the only light came from a pair of candles burning on a card table at the center of the room. Alongside the table were two metal folding chairs. Otherwise the room was empty of furnishings. Accompanying Kyoko here in the past, Sam had glanced through the doorway as she'd entered and seen that the room had boasted a tasteful, traditional décor, with rice paper walls providing privacy for readings, fine tatami floor coverings, and framed woodblock prints in the style of *ukiyo-e*, which were either authentic Edo period or damn good imitations. Now, the rice paper dividers were gone, the floors were cement, and the walls were bare. And the room smelled not of incense but of the broiled eel that was a staple in the neighborhood.

"After Pearl Harbor, the white men came and took everything from my business, claiming I was a witch," the old woman explained. Like her establishment, she too had lost any trappings of old-world dignity— where once she had greeted her customers in a traditional red *kimono* decorated with cranes, an elegant *obi*, and, for footwear, wooden *geta*, she now wore a housecoat and slippers that looked like they'd come mail order from Sears and Roebuck. Likewise, her once traditionally coiffed hair was now a bird's nest of grey, tangled strands. "I said to the white men," she continued, emphatically, 'Look around, you fools! Do you see any foxes here? I am no *kitsune-tsukai*.'"

Sumida knew from his study of art history that the fox was a common familiar of witches in Japanese mythology.

"'I am *uranaishi*, a fortune-teller,' I said to them," she continued. "But they admitted no difference. One of them wanted to beat me to death right here, 'a soldier of God putting down a demon,' he said. But the others reminded him that they'd come here to do Christian work. So they just destroyed or stole everything I owned."

"But you still live upstairs?"

"Where else would I go, young man?"

He looked at the folding table. "And you still do work for people?"

She surveyed him silently, as if once more appraising the likelihood that he was here to hurt or arrest her. After a moment, she held out her wrinkled palm. "The ten dollars," she said. "But, before you offer it to me, you must tell me why you're doing so."

"I want answers to questions," he said, before extending the sawbuck. She took it. "Good."

"Is that part of the clairvoyant process?" he asked, attempting to allow no cynicism or even doubt into his voice. "My spelling out exactly what I want from you like that?"

She shook her head. "Foolish boy. . . . It's a legal defense against entrapment," she answered. "Provided there *are* such things as legal defenses anymore. . . . Are there?"

"Legal defenses?"

She nodded. "I wouldn't know as I don't venture outside much anymore."

He considered. "Frankly, I don't know either."

She motioned him toward the card table and folding chairs.

"Thank you," he said as he sat down, placing his palms on the cheap table.

She sat opposite him. "Do not thank me unless you feel you have reason to do so *after* your reading."

"Fair enough," he said.

"Fairness, hah!" she laughed. "I hope that is not what you are here for. Fate is not fair. Just look around this room, for example. And look into your own heart, which has been wounded and worried so that it has brought you here, even as a nonbeliever."

He brightened. "You remember I was a nonbeliever? That it was my wife who came here and . . ."

"No," she interrupted. "I have never seen you before."

"Then how did you know I was a nonbeliever?" he asked.

"Your face gives you away," she answered, venturing a small smile. "One doesn't have to be a *uranaishi* to see that. So this is my first advice to you: do not take up poker."

Great, he thought. *Transparent. Not exactly an asset for a PI.* He wanted to change the subject, to return to the matter at hand. "What technique will you use for your reading?" he asked.

"I was once a practitioner of *Bokusen*," she answered.

"What is that?"

"A way of determining the divine will," she said. "And, in the process, of foretelling the future."

"How does it work?"

"I heat a tortoise shell until it cracks, at which time I interpret the crack," she said.

Sumida knew she had used this technique with Kyoko.

"But the white men took away everything," she added. "Tortoise shells too."

"So where does that leave us?"

"It leaves me *here*, stranded."

He said nothing.

She leaned toward him. "If what you're actually asking is what alternate technique I will use now that I have no tools, the answer is *Tengenjutsu*."

"Which is?"

"Let me ask the questions, young man."

He waited.

She looked at him for a long time, her milky eyes straining in the flickering light as if to discern some meaning from his face alone. He tried not to look away, but he failed to hold her gaze when their eyes met.

"What is your birthday?" she asked.

He told her.

"That is incorrect."

He removed his wallet from his back pocket, placing it on the table. "I can show you my driver's license."

She shook her head, then reached across the table and touched his hands. But only for a moment. . . .

She pulled away from him as if she had touched a live wire.

"You *have* no birthday," she said, her voice betraying confusion, revulsion, and even fear.

"That's impossible."

"You did not come here to learn your future," she continued, her eyes widening. "No, you've come because you want me to tell you what kind of creature you are!"

"Creature?" he muttered. "I just . . ."

She held her palm up to silence him. Taking his wallet, she pulled all of its contents out and onto the card table, spreading the cards and IDs and little pieces of paper as if mixing up a pile of children's pick-up sticks. "These are all worthless," she said, almost to herself. "Like you, they have no origin in this world. They do not belong." She brushed the empty leather wallet off the table, hard enough that it banged against the big, blackened window at the front of her ruined business. Then she ran her hands back and forth on the tabletop, scattering the cards and IDs. "Useless, all!"

They fluttered around the table.

Sumida did not move, shocked by her vehemence.

When the cards and papers settled onto the cement floor, one card remained on the table: the business card from Dr. Shinoda, with the dental appointment written on the back.

"This is the only reality you possess," she said, indicating the card.

With the name Henry Czernicek written on the back, it was actually the only document in his wallet that he knew for a fact was fraudulent.

"That card is all you need," she continued.

He picked it up. "A dental appointment?" he asked, testing her with sarcasm.

She ignored his taunt. Her eyes bored into his. "All that is left for you is to do whatever it is you're here to do."

"And what is that?"

"I don't know, but you do."

He put the dentist's card in his shirt pocket. "But why is this happening? There has to be an explanation."

"Only fools seek for explanations." She stood, holding out the ten-dollar bill he'd given her. "I've done nothing for you. Take back your money."

He shook his head. "You've been a great help."

"Take it!" she snapped, before dropping it on the table. "How can I have done something for you when there *is no you*?" Without further hesitation, she scrambled out of the room and up the stairs to her second-floor apartment. He heard her door close and a series of locks slip into place.

He sat for a moment.

He looked at the mess on the floor—the detritus of his wallet. He considered gathering it up again.

But she was right.

It was no use to him.

❧

Excerpt from chapter eleven of *The Orchid and the Secret Agent*, a novel by William Thorne
    Metropolitan Modern Mysteries, Inc., New York, N.Y., 1945

. . . Jimmy settled in the passenger seat of the Cadillac, which Mr. Barratt steered south on Central Avenue, past the last of the bank buildings in the downtown district, and into one of the Negro neighborhoods. Here, the jazz clubs were as vibrant as any in the entire United States. Jimmy loved jazz. Big bands were his favorite: Tommy Dorsey, Glenn Miller, Wayne King, Freddie Martin, Sammy Kaye. . . . And he also appreciated the Negro musicians, beginning with Duke Ellington's orchestra and including the edgy, experimental quartets and quintets who played the clubs that lined the half-dozen blocks through which Mr. Barratt drove the Cadillac now. Passing the *Club Alabam*, which Jimmy had visited once with Joe and a few of Joe's more open-minded police colleagues, he wondered if he'd ever hear jazz again? Or any kind of music? After what Mr. Barratt had said a moment before, he considered it a long shot.

"Are you listening to me, Jimmy?" Mr. Barratt asked from the driver's seat.

It was just the two of them in the car.

"I heard what you said," Jimmy replied. "I was just thinking about jazz."

"Jazz? Why?"

Mr. Barratt had rendezvoused with Jimmy at eight o'clock a few miles north of this neighborhood in a pay parking lot near, of all places, the Little Tokyo enclave. Before that, Mr. Barratt had said over the telephone that there'd been a "minor change of plans," which he'd explain to Jimmy on their drive down to the Pike Amusement Park in Long

Beach. Jimmy had imagined that Mr. Barratt would employ a driver and perhaps a bodyguard. He'd been surprised the two of them were alone. Now, he understood why.

"Jazz is an American art form," Jimmy answered. "It's one of a thousand things that this country can do unlike any other country in the world. One of a thousand reasons that a man should not hesitate to give his life for the USA."

Mr. Barratt kept his eyes fixed, concentrating on the barely sufficient glow cast by the car's masked headlights on the avenue ahead. "I didn't ask you to die for your country but to kill for it."

"I understand," Jimmy said, though he suspected that he stood little chance of surviving the new mission.

"Do you, Jimmy?"

"I understand that it's my place to follow orders."

"That's not true, Jimmy," Mr. Barratt answered, still staring straight ahead. "Orders are for the military. You're a civilian. This is a democracy. You have the right to say no. What you've been doing for your government and country has been especially appreciated because you never had to do any of it. And that's true of this mission as well. Doubly so. Just say the word and I'll turn this car around."

"You know I'll never say that word."

"Yes, I do know that," Mr. Barratt admitted. "But it's important to me that you understand *why* your mission's changed. Look, after your dispatching of those bullying hooligans in the alley outside that diner . . . well, owing to the number of witnesses, even *we* couldn't keep it out of the press."

"But I'm not a Jap," Jimmy protested.

"Yeah, tell that to the newspapers," Mr. Barratt replied. "Have you seen the late edition?"

Jimmy shook his head.

"'Mysterious Jap Spy Bests America's Youth,'" Mr. Barratt quoted. "Six unconscious college boys, four of whom play offensive line for UCLA . . . All this right in downtown LA. . . . If this city wasn't on the verge of panic before, it is now. Our citizens need reassurance. Just imagine if word had leaked about the three bloody murders! That's why there was little or no opposition among the leadership, who gathered again at my office in just the last hour, to changing your mission from one of infiltration to assassination. The truth is, I don't think our Military Intelligence colleagues realized quite how proficient you are at . . . well, violence. And so it was decided that stopping this Orchid right now, before she kills again, is more important than your infiltrating her organization to play the long game."

Jimmy looked out his side window. The wood-frame houses along Central Avenue spilled soft yellow light. Families inside . . . *Assassination is different than giving a beating*, he thought. But he didn't say it. He thought of the Tennyson poem. His was not to question why . . . "I understand the mission, sir."

Mr. Barratt said nothing, but waited to hear more.

"I'm sure you considered sending military into the Pike tonight to get her," Jimmy said.

"Sure, we considered it. But the use of massive force poses problems. First, we don't know that the Orchid will actually be at the fortune-teller booth. That location could just be a contact point for a subsequent location, so our showing up in force might only result in the arrest of a minor underling while serving to tip off the Orchid to our pursuit. No, we need you to play along as necessary to get close to the Orchid."

"To kill her," Jimmy muttered.

"Yes."

Jimmy understood.

"It's possible, even probable, that they'll search and disarm you when you enter her presence," Mr. Barratt said. "But among the many reasons we chose you for this operation is your capacity to put your *Taekwondo* to swift and deadly purpose."

Yes, that was something Jimmy could do, but he stayed silent.

"You're disturbed," Mr. Barratt observed, sympathetically.

"It's just new to me," Jimmy admitted. "I'm a PI, and I've gone undercover plenty against the Yakuza and the Tong. I've defended myself when I was called to do so. Yeah, I've killed bad guys before.

Quite a few. But assassination? That just takes me a minute or two to get used to."

"I understand," Mr. Barratt said.

"Thank you."

"Look, we've still got a ways to go before we get to Long Beach, right? If you're not comfortable with this reassignment by then, we'll call it off."

Jimmy didn't even dignify the offer with an answer. Of course he wouldn't be comfortable with the *idea* of assassination by the time they got to Long Beach. But neither would he say no to his country, especially when the threat against its citizens was so real, so vile. Everything Mr. Barratt had said about the Orchid was true. She had to be stopped, now. What difference did his state-of-mind make? Not a hill of beans. So he reached for the radio, clicking it on. "Let's find some jazz," he said to Mr. Barratt.

"You choose the station, Jimmy."

❧

Excerpt from a letter March 1, 1943:

. . . appreciate his thoughtful moments. But having Jimmy visit his family in Glendale, after leaving the diner in downtown LA, to wrestle with his conscience over his new assignment to assassinate the Orchid, slows the action considerably. Your reader is going to be quite anxious by this point to get to the amusement park, so I think it neither advisable nor necessary that we visit Jimmy's boyhood home or meet his father, however wise the old man's counsel. Actually, I suspect some of Jimmy's soul searching in his "homecoming" chapters is far more reflective of <u>your</u> character, my sensitive friend, than his. For

example, when he says, "I set out to do
good things, to speak for the quiet, little
man whose voice is otherwise nothing more
than the mere droning of a gnat in the face
of the powers-that-be," I can't help but
think of the reservations you've expressed
to me about the direction your book has
taken since the outbreak of the war, your
yearning to write the unpublishable Sumida
story instead of what is commercially and
politically viable. And I also know that
with the recent passing of your own father,
God rest his soul, you may have indulged in
some understandable role-playing, allowing
Jimmy to voice concerns with <u>his</u> father
that you'd like to voice with yours. All
very understandable.

Well, I don't presume to know what your
father would tell you about whatever reservations persist for you. But, as your
editor, I must remind you that the integrity
of your character, Jimmy Park, is seriously
threatened whenever you put your own words
into his mouth at the expense of <u>his</u> own
words and thoughts. That's right, <u>his own</u>.
After all, as you've speculated in a previous note, properly conceived characters
achieve a kind of independent Life, which
the author must honor rather than merely
presume to create. So, in this light, are
you allowing Jimmy his life?

Additionally, and somewhat less esoter-
ically, your professionalism should insure
that you provide pace sufficient to your
"spy novel" that readers will want to keep
turning the pages. This is a basic require-
ment. If, instead, you allow self-doubt and

moral confusion (despite my numerous assur-
ances to you about the inherently good-
hearted nature of our project) to interfere
with the basic requirements of good sto-
rytelling—coherent character and compel-
lingly paced plot—then you are failing as
a writer and that leaves you . . . where?
Nowhere, Takumi.

Now, I'm not suggesting that Jimmy need
be callous about things. Perhaps you can
condense the two chapters you've currently
set in Glendale into one conversation
with Mr. Barratt in the car while trav-
eling <u>toward</u> the amusement park? I'm not
asking that Jimmy be cardboard. Sure, give
him feelings. Just be quite certain that
they're his and not yours.

Forgive my vehemence on this, please.
It's just that your project and your well-
being in general have come to mean so much
to me these past months. How could they not?
In our personal lives we've each suffered
incalculable losses (yes, my husband remains
MIA). But you and I are bound together as
comrades by a game fellow named Jimmy Park.
You created him. Now, he's his own man. So
grab some of his reckless enthusiasm when
you need it. And share it with me, please.

Cut the stuff in Glendale. Let's get to
the shoot 'em up.

Affectionately,

Maxine

THE REVISED—CHAPTER SEVEN

And oftentimes, to win us to our harm,
The instruments of darkness tell us truths...

—William Shakespeare

It was just past eight when Sumida entered the lobby of the Barclay Hotel on Fourth and Main. In the initial hours after his inquiries at the dentist's office and with the soothsayer in Little Tokyo, he'd wandered the downtown, considering what to do when he met Czernicek. His various plans all ended the same—his gaining satisfaction. But he needed proof. He needed a confession. He settled on a plan. Nonetheless, in the early evening, with time left to kill, other questions persisted. So he had returned to the library, this time to the metaphysics section, 110 by Dewey Decimal reckoning, which seemed one place he might find an explanation for the strange dislocation of the past day. The soothsayer had told him seeking such answers was strictly for fools. Well, he *was* a fool.

How else could he have arrived in these circumstances?

Besides, haunting the library shelves was better than wandering the street. It felt familiar. He was an academic, after all. And he needed something to take his mind off the coming confrontation with Czernicek. (If he was a drinker this would have involved a bar, if he was a womanizer a brothel, but he was neither.)

Unfortunately, his library research turned up only the concept of the *doppelganger*, a German word for an apparition who is an exact double of a living person. There were reputed examples from history.

The poet Shelley claimed that on an Italian shore he had once met his doppelganger, who silently pointed toward the Mediterranean. Not long after, Shelley drowned in the same sea. The French author de Maupassant claimed to have been aided by his doppelganger, who came to him late in his life to dictate a story. Shortly before her death, Queen Elizabeth I of England saw her doppelganger lying portentously on the royal bed. The poet John Donne met his wife's doppelganger while he was in Paris and she was giving birth in England. Being of a bookish sensibility, Sumida absorbed the superstitious accounts with interest, attempting to connect the phenomenon with his own experience. Might *he* be a doppelganger? No, his friend Tony Fortuna would have recognized him, as being recognizable was the defining characteristic of a doppelganger. Besides, if Sumida were a doppelganger then it should have been his "authentic" self, rather than a stranger, who lived in his Echo Park bungalow. It all came to nothing.

He was no more a doppelganger than he was a ghost or an urban sprite.

Sumida left the library with no more understanding than he'd had when he entered it. His research skills were worthless to him now. He didn't know what he was, except flesh and blood.

The soothsayer was right.

But he would be a fool no longer. Instead, he would do what he was called upon to do by his own small, still voice, leaving the desire for understanding to the babbling, drunken prophets who lived in their own filth on Fifth Street, the infamous Nickel. Still, he couldn't help considering how dire a man's situation was when he discovered himself disappointed to realize that he was not an apparition but that he and the world he inhabited were both real, if unfathomable.

The walk from the library to the Barclay Hotel was short.

By the time he passed through the revolving door, he'd moved on from Shelley, de Maupassant, Queen Elizabeth I, and John Donne. Instead, he considered Hamlet, who, like Sumida, suffered from sometimes wanting to know *too much*. Now Sumida thought that "To be or not to be" mightn't be the essential question. There need be no questions at all. Instead, the Dane may have gotten it right simply with this: *Oh, from this time forth, my thoughts be bloody, or be nothing worth.*

He approached the front desk clerk, a bespectacled man who stood at least six and a half feet tall but couldn't have weighed much more than Sumida himself. "I have an appointment with one of your guests, Henry Czernicek," Sumida said.

The clerk glanced down at the guest register, then back at the wall of keys.

"Mr. Czernicek is out."

Sumida nodded. "I'll wait." He started toward the modest but comfortably furnished lobby.

"Not here you won't," the night clerk said.

Sumida stopped and turned. "What?"

"No Japs hanging around the lobby."

Sumida knew he could reach over the counter and pull the string bean over it, then break him in two over his knee. But what was the percentage in that? "Look, he'll be here any minute."

"Then you won't have to wait outside too long."

Sumida didn't have to wait outside at all, as Czernicek just then entered the lobby, his coat fluttering about him as if he were Doug Fairbanks. In his hand, he carried a file. "We need to go up to my room," he said, approaching Sumida but not offering his hand.

Sumida wouldn't have shaken it anyway.

"We've got things to discuss," Czernicek continued.

"Yes we do," Sumida affirmed.

Czernicek strode to the front desk. "512," he said to the string bean clerk, who handed over the key.

"You going to take that Jap up to your room?" the clerk asked.

"He's a Chink," Czernicek answered. "Don't sweat it."

The desk clerk didn't like it. But he turned back to a novel he had open behind the counter.

Sumida and Czernicek were silent in the open grill elevator.

"You can take a seat over there, near the window," Czernicek said, after he opened his room door and flipped on the light.

Sumida entered.

Czernicek closed the door after himself and casually set the file on top of a weathered dresser. "I've got to take a piss," he said, walking into the bathroom. He didn't bother closing the door.

Sumida did not sit but stood, waiting, listening to the heavy stream from the john. He took a deep breath to steady his nerves and checked the pistol in the back waistband of his trousers—the .38 Special he had taken the night before from Tony Fortuna, who'd previously taken it from the unconscious hulk on the sofa.

The toilet flushed.

Czernicek emerged into the hotel room, still zipping his trousers. "Better now."

Sumida wasn't going to waste any time. He stepped toward Czernicek, extending the business card he had taken from Dr. Shinoda's dental office with the appointment scribbled on the back. "I just found this lying here beside the bed," he lied. "It must have fallen out of your jacket."

Czernicek took the card and looked at it. Then he slipped it casually into his trousers pocket.

"He's your dentist," Sumida said, allowing for no denial.

Czernicek's eyes narrowed. His thought registered on his movie-star face: had he allowed a moment's lapse, carelessness, exposure? His expression turned to one of aggression. "I didn't say anything about him being my dentist."

"But you took the card without a second thought."

"Look, what kind of game are you playing at, Sumida?"

"Earlier, you mentioned using 'cut-rate' Japanese dentistry," Sumida calmly explained.

"Lots of people go to this Shinoda," Czernicek said.

"We're not talking about Dr. Shinoda."

Czernicek waited.

"That office is where Kyoko used to work," Sumida continued. "But you already knew that, Czernicek. Everybody knew. It was at the public inquest. What wasn't public, however, was that you'd been a patient of Dr. Shinoda and that you met my wife there."

Czernicek sighed as if bored.

Sumida continued. "I don't know how you charmed her. The usual ways, I'd guess. Good looks. Cop. But you ought to know that she was already unhappy at home. With me. I'll admit that. So don't pat yourself too much on the back for having taken her away."

"I didn't take nobody."

"She was a beautiful woman," Sumida said. "I commend your taste."

"She *was* a beautiful woman," Czernicek snapped, his patience exhausted. "Too damn good for you. Too damn good for any of you. I wonder, how is it that Jap women are so much better looking than their men? I don't understand how there're even any purebred Jap babies, considering the sorry ass Jap men your women have to fuck. But your wife didn't mean anything to me. Understand? I got chippies on every block of this city. You met one today at lunch. The truth is, I can't even keep them straight. And why would I bother?"

"So she didn't mean more to you than any of the others?"

"That's right. She was just another piece of ass. An exotic one, at least."

"So why did you kill her?"

"Kill her?" Czernicek laughed and sat down on the bed. "You've completely gone around the bend."

Sumida knew Czernicek was armed and dangerous. Now, having broached the subject of Kyoko's murder, this was no longer a time for subtlety. Reaching into his back waistband, Sumida withdrew the .38, pointing it at Czernicek's head. "Don't move," he said. He was glad that his voice betrayed little of the anxiety he felt. Glad too that his hand was steady. Until now, he hadn't been sure either would be the case. He sorted through the books and movies he'd studied for what to say next. Spade, the Continental Op, even Nick Charles . . . "With two fingers gently remove your weapon from its holster and drop it on the carpet, kicking it toward me."

Czernicek grinned. "Which is it, Sumida? 'Don't move?' Or 'remove my weapon?' See, your orders kind of contradict each other."

"Don't get smart with me, Czernicek."

"Hey, you're the professor," Czernicek said. "The smart one. I'm the good looking one."

Sumida motioned with the .38. "Remove your goddamn gun. Drop it on the carpet and kick it toward me. And if you try anything funny you should be assured that even an amateur couldn't miss your pretty face from this range." Sumida felt a surge of confidence. "And I'm not as much an amateur as you may think."

Sighing, Czernicek did as Sumida asked.

Without looking down, Sumida kicked Czernicek's handgun further out of reach, under the bed.

"Kyoko *was* something special to you, whatever you claim," Sumida said, his hand hot on the big gun. "Otherwise she would still be alive. Just like your string of waitresses are alive. But Kyoko wasn't like them."

Czernicek shook his head. "I don't like to disappoint you, but she was *nothing* to me."

Sumida waited. He held the gun.

"The truth is," Czernicek said after a moment, "I hadn't thought of her since we put her file in the cold cases a few weeks after the crime. It was only seeing you that brought her to mind at all."

"That's a lie."

Czernicek looked away, as if frustrated. "I slept with your wife," he said. "Sorry. But even you admit I didn't break up your already failing marriage." His manner turned more reasonable. "So why don't you put down the gun. I'll stand up right here and let you take your best shot at me, right in the kisser. Knock me out cold if you can. I deserve it. Man to man. Then we can get past this woman thing and back to the pressing matter, which is that you and I *don't seem to exist* in this place, which I used to think was just Los Angeles."

Sumida wouldn't allow himself to be distracted, even by the existential confusion that had characterized his last hours. "You lie about my wife."

"Why do you keep saying that?"

"Because when I walked into the periodicals room this morning at the library I was told that you'd already checked out the newspaper for January 12, 1941, the day the story broke about Kyoko's murder."

That seemed to take Czernicek aback.

"Oh, it didn't strike me as suspicious at first," Sumida continued. "It should have, but everything seemed so disorienting then. My mind's cleared now, even if I still don't understand how things work with you and me and the rest of the world." He shook his head. "That world stuff's a real pisser, huh? It's like we two were excised from the universe and now we've been dropped back into some variation of it in where we never existed. I don't understand why. I don't have to. I don't care. Because I'm standing here now just thinking about that newspaper. And I can't imagine why you'd request that particular day's edition if you'd 'forgotten' all about Kyoko's existence until you saw me, as you claim?" He didn't wait for an answer. "Sure, you were confused back in the periodicals room. You wanted to know if the murder you'd committed had followed you, now that everything else had seemed to fall away. And you were probably relieved to learn that it hadn't. But there I was. You should have killed me the minute you saw me. Before I got clear in my mind. But now it's too late. Now, I know you killed her."

"You're insane."

"No. It makes sense. The white man who nobody at the hotels recognized . . . It was you. And this is LA. So who's going to testify against a police detective, especially when he's the one asking the questions, heading up the 'investigation'? Who's dumb enough to think anything but an early grave would await such testimony? So you got a free pass. Except from me."

"So what if you're right?" Czernicek asked calmly. "What are you going to do? Shoot me?"

Sumida nodded, equally calm.

"That would be a mistake."

"Why?"

Czernicek laughed. He gestured with his chin toward the dresser, where he'd dropped the file that he'd carried into the hotel. "Because it's possible you're right and wrong at the same time."

Sumida waited.

Czernicek shrugged. "I killed her down on the docks. You're right about her being kind of special. But she'd had her fill of me. For all I know, the little Geisha wanted to go back to you. And I didn't like that. I didn't have to tolerate that. So I shot her in the head. Quick, painless."

It took all the will Sumida possessed not to pull the trigger right then.

"Just a splash off the dock and she was gone for somebody else to fish out," Czernicek continued. "Nothing new down at the harbor. The thing barely even makes news when it's somebody with brown skin or black skin or yellow skin. So you'd be right to shoot me dead now, except for one thing."

Sumida waited. He'd be damned if he'd ask.

Czernicek broke first. "This evening I got into my old office at the station, flashing my badge and claiming to be new, since nobody recognized me. But my key still worked. It'll come as no surprise that the office wasn't mine anymore. I searched it anyway. Turns out the place belongs to the head of some special anti-Jap task force working with the Feds. Spy stuff. National security. I used another of my keys on the filing cabinet." Again, Czernicek gestured with his chin toward the file. "I borrowed that file because you'd be interested, buddy."

"I thought you were going to tell me why I shouldn't shoot you dead right now."

"Because your wife is alive," Czernicek said.

Sumida froze. He wouldn't be taken in.

"Just look at the file," Czernicek said.

Sumida approached the detective, keeping the .38 pointed at the big man's head. He wasn't going to get so close that Czernicek might take a swing at him; rather, he drew just close enough to kick Czernicek on the point of his chin, sending him sprawling backward over the length of the bed and hard against the wall, unconscious. Sumida dragged the man to the radiator. There, he removed Czernicek's keys and handcuffs and bound him to metal piping. Last, he stuffed the bastard's mouth with a hand towel in case he woke and tried to call for help.

Sumida still planned to kill him.

But first the file . . .

He opened it. On top was a photo.

It was Kyoko, dressed in a luxurious gown that Sumida could never imagine being able to buy for her. And her hair was done up in an uncharacteristically extravagant, traditional fashion. But there was no mistaking her face. She was as beautiful as he remembered—her skin silk, her cheek bones and chin somehow imperially strong without diminishing her soft femininity, her hair streaked with the line of white that she'd had since early childhood. True, in this photograph her expression was one Sam had not seen before—determined, heedless. But the face was unmistakable. Written in grease pencil across the front of the 8X10 were the words: "The Orchid." He didn't understand the reference.

The photo was dated: 1/19/42. Just a few days ago . . .

Typed papers clipped to the photo suggested the Feds believed she was an enemy to America.

That was impossible.

Kyoko was no traitor, whatever melodramatic name they'd assigned to her. And there was worse—the documents outlined a plan for her assassination, scheduled for this night at the Pike in Long Beach.

Czernicek's killing would keep.

Sumida grabbed the detective's wallet—he'd need money for a cab and might be able to put the police ID to some use. Then he raced from the room, locking the door behind him, and descended the five flights down the stairway. He lowered his hat over his eyes, knowing the eight o'clock curfew complicated his movements. But he wasn't going to let that stop him. When he got to the lobby, he slipped unseen past the clerk and into the blacked-out LA streets. In such darkness, who'd even be able to pick him out as Japanese?

He wondered: what would a working amusement park be like with most of its lights dimmed or shut off altogether? All shadows and noise. It would provide just the cover he needed, he thought.

Excerpt from chapter twelve of *The Orchid and the Secret Agent*, a novel
by William Thorne
    Metropolitan Modern Mysteries, Inc., New York, N.Y., 1945

... On Saturday nights, the Pike amusement park was lively and
crowded, even with ninety percent of the lights turned off in accordance
with black-out measures. This precaution was mandated nightly
for coastal businesses and residences, as a glowing coastline could
silhouette Navy ships and make them vulnerable to submarine attack.
Most inland areas enacted full black-out procedures only when alerted
by air-raid sirens. Now, Mr. Barratt pulled the Cadillac to the curb on
Ocean Avenue near the entrance, which Jimmy knew from previous
recreational visits featured a glorious string of electric bulbs, known as
the Walk of a Thousand Lights, that led down the boardwalk to the
midway. Tonight, there was no such electric marvel. Still, the sound
of calliope music and the roar and swoosh of the big, wooden roller
coaster, the Cyclone Racer, were audible inside Mr. Barratt's Cadillac,
even with the windows rolled up. Having visited the Pike many times as
a child, Jimmy had warm memories of the place. He suspected tonight
would resemble those carefree days in no way whatsoever.

    "Naturally, you'll recognize the Orchid, if and when you see her,"
Mr. Barratt said, shifting the car into park. "Judging from her recent
murder spree, she doesn't shy away from flamboyance. And even if she
tried to conceal her identity ... well, that streak of white in her hair is
an easily identifiable detail."

    "She might have dyed it, sir."

    Mr. Barratt shook his head. "She wants you to recognize her
because she wants you to join her. She's proud of all the killing she's
done. That's why I don't think she'll disguise her identity for a meeting
with you. Not after providing you with such vivid and bloody clues to
her location."

    "But why would she want to recruit me, Mr. Barratt? I'm not a Jap."

    "Perhaps she knows about your association with us and sees you as
a perfect double agent."

"But why would she believe I'd betray you? I'm an American through and through. And even if that weren't enough, you know what the Japs did to my homeland."

"Yes, I know," Mr. Barratt said, looking away as if painfully considering the Jap atrocities practiced for years on the Korean peninsula. He turned back to his agent. "I honestly don't know how she thinks she'll turn you to her side, Jimmy. But she must have her reasons, deluded as they may be."

Jimmy said nothing.

"Threats maybe, or enticements . . ." Mr. Barratt started.

"Mean nothing to me," Jimmy interrupted.

"Good," Mr. Barratt said. "Then you won't hesitate. Just put one between her eyes."

Jimmy nodded. They'd been over it before.

"And there's one other thing I wanted to mention before you go, Jimmy."

"Okay," Jimmy said, though he wasn't sure he really wanted to hear more. The phrase of Mr. Barratt's that resonated in Jimmy's head, spoken for the first time moments before, was "right between her eyes . . ." Jimmy was an experienced undercover detective and an international operative, but assassination still did not sit easily with him. So he reminded himself of the heinous crimes the Orchid had committed in just the last twenty-four hours—the bloody slaughter of three innocent men just because their names, taken together, formed a message she wanted to convey. And her personal violence was the least of it, according to Mr. Barratt. She was also the treacherous brains behind the entire West Coast Jap spy ring, whose mission was to weaken American defenses for an impending invasion of the homeland. No ordinary dame . . . Still, Jimmy had never killed a woman. Sensing the hesitation, Mr. Barratt had suggested he think of her less as a woman and more as a female cobra, poised to strike. "Do we allow gentlemanly considerations to interfere with our dispatching of threatening, poisonous snakes?" he'd asked. "Even female ones?" The rationale had made sense to Jimmy. But he wasn't sure he wanted to hear more from Mr. Barratt. Rather, he just wanted to get out of the car and get on with his mission.

"It's about the Orchid's bodyguard, this *Fantomu*, or Phantom," Mr. Barratt said.

Talk of the Phantom had been noticeably absent until now.

"I've discussed the matter with my most trusted team of analysts," Mr. Barratt continued.

Jimmy was struck by the strange juxtaposition of talking about killers while, outside, the cheerful background sounds of calliope music and young people's happy cries of excitement on the darkened Cyclone Racer echoed through the night.

"Are you listening to me, Jimmy?" Mr. Barratt inquired, moving his hand from the steering wheel to rest companionably on Jimmy's shoulder.

Jimmy nodded. He was not distracted by the sounds of the Pike. Rather, he was entering into a state of mind he'd come to trust—one of hypersensitivity, not only to his external surroundings but also to the thoughts that fluttered through his mind. In this state, he could take in far more than he did in his ordinary, walking-around frame of mind. He had practiced no Oriental discipline to develop the state but just seemed to have been born with it. When thus engaged, almost nothing could get past him. The sensitivity had saved his life many times. And the familiar frame of mind was arriving now, right on time. "Please continue, sir."

Mr. Barratt removed his hand from Jimmy's shoulder. "As yet, there have been no sightings of this 'Phantom;' nonetheless, we doubt he has ever abandoned his post as the Orchid's bodyguard. The fact of his *seeming* absence suggests that he exhibits none of the flamboyant appearance of his dark lady, but, likely, looks perfectly ordinary, altogether unthreatening, thereby achieving a kind of invisibility while in plain sight. Unfortunately, we can offer you no further intelligence regarding identifying marks of this dangerous creature. Only this final reminder for you to assume always that he is someplace close."

"But he *will* be Japanese, right?" Jimmy inquired.

Mr. Barratt nodded. "Unfortunately, however, the dimmed lights on the Pike will make it difficult to pick out the particulars of anyone's face. I don't know why the Army allows them to keep the place open at all, blacked-out or not. Public morale, I suppose. But what it leaves us with tonight are little more than shadows. And any one of them might be the Phantom."

Jimmy thought he could pretty well rule out the babies in perambulators. "I'll stay aware," he said.

"Of course, the chaotic darkness is probably why the Orchid chose this place as a rendezvous point," Mr. Barratt said, handing a tiny flashlight to Jimmy.

Jimmy turned on the flashlight. "This barely gives off as much light as a candle."

"Well, that's what everybody at the Pike'll be carrying. It's how you keep a coastal amusement park open during a war."

Jimmy nodded. "Must be high times for pickpockets."

"Pickpockets aren't our problem," Mr. Barratt said, offering his hand to shake.

Jimmy shook it.

Both men's palms were as dry as the Sahara.

Jimmy climbed out of the car, closing the door after him.

Mr. Barratt pulled away, disappearing around the first corner.

Jimmy watched him go. Now he was alone.

After a moment, he checked the handgun holstered beneath his coat and then crossed the street toward the boardwalk. Music and voices, rather than glimmering strings of powerful bulbs, indicated the way through the entrance and to the midway, which featured long-remembered concessions, barely distinguishable now in the dim light, but still operational. There was nothing like American tenacity in the face of a threat. Hundreds of weak flashlight spots (hardly beams) fluttered from instruments barely larger than a fountain pen, those wielded by children hovering like fireflies at waist level. He used his candle-power light to navigate past Sea Side Souvenir Photography, McGruder Salt Water Taffy, the Plunge bathhouse (closed now, but a crowd favorite in summer), pitch and skill games of such wide variety that their only common trait was their deceptive simplicity ("Three balls for a nickel, a child could do it!"). All lit by barely more than a lantern power's worth of electricity. But the place remained lively and *noisy*. Sound made no difference to Jap bombers. So the Cyclone Racer, the big wooden coaster, provided a continual railroad rattle of wooden ties and choruses of screaming riders, the combination of which Jimmy thought could be useful if he needed to conceal the sounds of violence.

But being Oriental himself, he occasionally encountered hard looks from passersby whose flashlight beams happened upon his face. He hardly blamed them. In the push and jangle of the crowd, how could they know he was Korean, rather than a Jap? Being the object of derisive looks and comments didn't make his job any easier. He bought a tall cotton candy that he held in front of his face as he proceeded. Among all the shadowed figures, it seemed to work as concealment.

Of course, the Orchid was expecting him, regardless of precautions. This was no stealth operation.

Rather, it was a perverse business appointment (feigned) that would end with his killing his negotiating partner. Yes, killing her in the very midst of her lair . . . Likely surrounded by her underlings, or at least by the *Fantomu* . . .

In short, a suicide mission.

But that's what he'd signed on for. And considering the thousands of lives in the balance, his personal sacrifice seemed a worthwhile exchange. And if he were going to die he wouldn't mind dying here, where he'd been happy as a child. The Fun House, the Skooter (the indoor bumper cars), the Crazie Maze (a house of mirrors), the Super Trooper Umbrella Ride, the Sky Wheel . . .

On second thought, what a ridiculous place to die.

He turned and started up the pier, which was likewise lined with dimly lit attractions, food stalls, and concessions. He stopped in front of the Gypsy fortune-teller's establishment, a small, enclosed structure that bore the appearance of a Bohemian shack. A window box, displaying an electric candle, allowed no glimpse inside. A sign above the wooden door read: "Madame Belinsky—Authentic Gypsy Fortune-Teller."

This was the place.

He looked around him. All the passersby appeared ordinary. At least in so much as he could see them. But then whom did he expect to be looming on the crowded pier, Dr. Fu Manchu?

He took a deep breath and stepped to the door. There was no "Open" sign. No "Come In." Was he to knock? What if the fortune-teller had an ordinary customer inside, hearing right now about his or her golden future? But Jimmy didn't hesitate. He turned the knob and the door opened.

He walked in.

❧

Excerpt from a letter April 2, 1943:

. . . as one acquainted with loss. (Yes, my dear husband's body has been recovered and soon I'll be placing a gold star in the window of my apartment.) So I can relate to the pain you are feeling, Takumi. Of course, your girlfriend is not deceased, but, in some ways, having your heart rejected may sometimes be as painful as losing a loved one to a noble death. Who can weigh and compare feeling? Still, I must remind you that her recent letter to you should not be taken too personally, odd as that may sound at first. She is young and your being away in Manzanar these past thirteen months with no end in sight cannot help but be dis-couraging for her. And adding to the diffi-culty, of course, is that she is Caucasian and so all along (even in your happy times together, before the internment) she's had to keep your adventurous love a secret, an especially lonely situation for her. I say these things not to attempt to dismiss the pain you are feeling but to temper it with the certain knowledge that her breakup is not based on any shortcoming you possess or any neglectful behavior on your part. There are simply circumstances beyond our control and we must acknowledge them and, to the best of our ability, attempt to move forward even with our broken hearts.

For me, work is the best balm. Naturally, I have grief-ridden, terrible nights. I loved my man. But I find that coming in to work every day enables me to escape, at least for a few hours, the dark cloud of loss that otherwise hovers about the whole world these days. I don't know that it will be the same for you, but I am quite certain that doing nothing with yourself, succumbing to the depression that accompanies loss, is no answer. Knowing you as I do now, I believe that work will be a balm to you too. Your book's rapidly approaching deadline may actually be a blessing if it aids you in focusing your attention on your talents, your responsibilities, and your future.

I have found that if we can no longer put our passion into loving our sweethearts, then we must find other places to put it, otherwise we become broken people. That is not what I want for you, dear boy. Put your passion into your work. I thought your most recent submission (at the darkened amusement park) was among your best. I made virtually no marks with my blue pencil. I understand that you wrote it before receiving this recent, discouraging correspondence from

THE REVISED—CHAPTER EIGHT

*What do we truly look for in the face of our beloved if not,
above all else, redemption? And, frankly, what a forlorn
enterprise is that?*

—Greta Garbo in *Silver Screen Magazine*

I t was half past nine when Sumida paid the hack and climbed out onto
Ocean Avenue, across the street from the Pike. The cabbie, who had
brought Sumida here after curfew only after Sumida flashed Czernicek's
police badge and told the driver he was on official business, pulled
away from the curb. Watching the big Checker cab disappear into the
gloom, he reached back to touch the .38 Special he had slipped into the
waistband of his trousers. Then he turned toward the darkened seaside
amusement park, where, according to the police report that Czernicek
had stolen a few hours before, the Orchid was to be found in a fortune-
telling concession. The sound of calliope music, the roar and swoosh
of the big, wooden roller coaster, the Cyclone Racer, and the happy
exclamations of Saturday night revelers filled the night air. Sam had
fond memories of this place, having grown up only a few miles away.
He recalled that along the Walk of a Thousand Lights, which led to
the midway, you'd find Sea Side Souvenir Photography, McGruder Salt
Water Taffy, the Plunge bathhouse, and dozens of pitch and skill games
of such wide variety that their only common trait was their deceptive
simplicity. But this was no time for nostalgia. Besides, this wasn't the
same place with the Walk of a Thousand Lights shut off, along with the
lights on the Ferris wheel, the roller coaster, the midway, the pier, and

all the other rides and attractions. In all, the Pike gave off little more light than a scattering of tiny campfires around which hovered a thousand fireflies—useless to any Japanese planes approaching the mainland at ten thousand feet.

He started across the street.

❧

Excerpt from chapter thirteen of *The Orchid and the Secret Agent*, a novel by William Thorne
    Metropolitan Modern Mysteries, Inc., New York, N.Y., 1945

. . . Jimmy closed the door to Madame Belinsky's tiny, one-room establishment, shutting out much, but not all, of the racket of the crowded pier outside. Now, the only light came from the center of the shack, where a pair of candles flickered atop a round café table that was covered by a dark velvet cloth. Seated at the table, watching him, her appearance a play of shadows, was Madame Belinsky. Weathered and dark complexioned, her face *looked* like that of a real Gypsy, as did her lavishly layered clothing, headdress, and bejeweled neck and forearms.

"Will it be tarot cards or a palm reading?" she asked.

Her accent *sounded* Eastern European (though Jimmy's linguistic expertise did not extend to Slavic languages). Then again, the whole presentation might as easily be described as quintessentially "carny" as "authentic Gypsy mystic"—Jimmy wondered if there was any difference between the two anyway?

One thing was clear: she was not the Orchid.

"Tarot or palmistry?" she repeated.

Jimmy didn't answer but silently took in the room. The lavish decor suggested Madame Belinsky might have obtained her furnishings from props left over from the old silent movie, *The Sheik*.

"I like what you've done with the place," he said.

She seemed to miss his irony. "We Gypsies have had more than a millennium to develop a true sense of style."

"You're Madame Belinsky?"

"Who else would I be?"

Jimmy knew enough to be cautious when his questions were answered with other questions, even of the seemingly harmless, rhetorical variety.

"You still haven't answered *my* question, sir," Madame Belinsky pressed.

"About the means of fortune-telling?"

"What else?" Again, she answered with what *seemed* a harmless rhetorical question.

"I can't choose the method of divination, Madame Belinsky, because I'm not here to dictate terms." He assumed his words were being heard clandestinely by the Orchid. Likely, there was a microphone hidden somewhere in the small room. "I'm here tonight only to listen humbly to whatever propositions *you* offer, by whatever means you deem appropriate."

"Good answer," Madame Belinsky affirmed. "Sit down."

Jimmy sat at the small chair across the table from the soothsayer. "How much for a reading?"

Madame Belinsky smiled, her mouth revealing half-a-dozen gold teeth scattered among the rot. "Tonight's reading will be free of charge."

"That's very generous."

The smile disappeared as she shook her head. "I am not generous, but knowing. You see, should you return after tonight to learn more of your future, *then* remuneration will be quite substantial. Virtually all you can afford. Is that clear?" She didn't wait for an answer. "But, of course, you will return only if you deem worthwhile what I say to you tonight."

"That sounds pretty much like standard carnival patter, Madame," he said, dismissively. "The usual ruse. I expected something a little more personal. Even unique."

"Ah, you're a bold young man," she responded, rolling her eyes momentarily heavenward. "Brave. But it takes no soothsayer to see you're courageous. After all, an Oriental out after dark walking among hundreds of whites . . ."

"If you're a true seer, then you know I'm not Japanese," he interrupted.

"I didn't say you were," she sneered. "But you know well enough that there are many Caucasians who do not ask for ID to confirm your ancestry before beating you."

She was right.

"In fact, you had just such a close call earlier this evening," she added, looking him hard in the eye. "Yes, I see how your reminiscence of the confrontation colors your aura. And I can see the actual scene, six threatening hulks in an alley, imprinted upon the iris of your mystic third eye."

Initially, Jimmy wasn't impressed. Mr. Barratt had told him that the incident with the college boys was already in the news. But how could she know it had been Jimmy who'd beaten the six boys? Unless, perhaps, the Orchid's organization had sent the six in the first place and had been observing all along. . . . But turning a half-dozen American college boys to evil Japanese Imperialist collaboration? Impossible. Even his "mystic third eye" was a more likely explanation. In any case, he hadn't time to fret over parlor tricks. "Look, there's no need for you to waste my time with your usual hokum. I'm not just some sucker from the pier. You know that. So let's get down to business."

"But you have not yet chosen. Tarot or palmistry?"

The last thing he wanted was to give her the opportunity to ham it up with cards. "Palmistry," he said.

"Good. Give me your palms."

He extended his right arm, setting his hand palm up at the center of the small table.

"Both hands please."

This didn't feel right. But if the Orchid wanted him dead, she'd have finished the job by now. So he set his left hand palm up beside his right.

Madame Belinsky touched his hands, studying them as she lightly ran her index fingers along the creases in his palms. "I see great opportunity ahead for you," she said.

So this was how the offer to betray his country would be made, he speculated.

"Go on, Madame Belinsky."

But before she could say more, a loud explosion from far above rattled the pier and shook the Gypsy's tiny structure to its nuts and bolts. Startled, Jimmy pulled back his hands.

His first thought was that the Japs were bombing.

Two seconds later came another explosion and then another and another, accompanied by the unexpected roar and cheers of revelers along the midway and the pier. Suddenly, he understood. It was a fireworks display.

He sighed, relieved. Then his breath caught in his throat.

Fireworks during a black-out?

Besides, even before the war the Pike had only displayed fireworks on summer nights. He looked at his watch. It was almost ten p.m. Too late for many of the amusement park's prime clientele, children, who'd already been taken home. This made no sense.

Unless, of course, it was the work of the Orchid.

Had he simply been lured to the center of a bombing target?

Madame Belinsky raised her voice to be heard over the continuing explosive din. "Are you as distractible as a small child?" she inquired critically. "Will you be so weak as to allow a mere light show in the sky to distract you from our profound work in *here*!" She indicated with her hands that Jimmy was to return his palms to the table.

Meanwhile, the pier shuddered with each explosion.

The amusement park patrons roared their approval.

Jimmy raised his voice to be heard, even as he leaned toward Madame Belinsky. "Maybe we should wait until it's over."

She shook her head. "Give me your palms," she insisted, her voice screeching. "Now or never."

He did as she asked, returning his palms to the table.

The Gypsy woman resumed running her index fingers along the lines in his palms, silently.

Outside: "Boom! Boom! Boom!"

Then she looked up at him, grinning widely—all gold and rot.

That's when he felt the muzzle of a gun at the back of his head.

"Don't move, Jimmy Park," said a woman, with a sultry, unaccented voice. "I wouldn't want to have to put a hole in your head before we've even had the opportunity to meet properly."

It wasn't hard to guess whose voice it was.

Meanwhile, Madame Belinsky dexterously slapped a pair of handcuffs on Jimmy's exposed wrists.

He took a deep, steadying breath.

The game was on. It was early yet, he thought. First quarter . . .

But he was already losing.

"You used the fireworks as distraction," Jimmy observed, without turning his head.

"Yes," she answered. "They are quite expensive, but effective. Americans love loud noise and bright lights. It's like the Fourth of July out there tonight, ha! And by the time the authorities realize that the glittering extravaganza has not actually been arranged by the amusement park but by some mysterious benefactor, we'll be long gone."

"And the din allowed you to follow me through Madame Belinsky's front door," he speculated.

"We didn't use the *front* door." Her voice communicated both calm and sensuality. "No, we came in through a trapdoor beneath Madame Belinsky's old, blue Turkish rug."

Jimmy closed his eyes in frustration. He should have examined the room more closely before sitting down, he silently chided himself. But then he reflected: the point of the evening was to make contact with the Orchid.

And here she was.

Sure, there was a gun at his head, but nobody said it was going to be easy.

"The little trapdoor opens to a ladder that leads under the pier to a catwalk suspended eight or ten feet over the sea," she continued. "It's how we'll be going out. You'll see it soon enough, Mr. Park."

Two large Japs dressed in black, like burglars, approached from behind and took hold of Jimmy's arms.

"How many of you are there in this little shack?" Jimmy asked, unable to turn around to look. "Are we crammed in here like sardines?"

"Just us three," the Orchid answered, pressing the gun harder against his skull. "My associates, Shinji and Kento, and me."

"Us *four*," Madame Belinsky corrected.

The big Japs gripped Jimmy's arms harder, securing him firmly.

The Orchid lowered the gun from Jimmy's head and stepped around the table. At last, Jimmy got a good look at her. She wore a slinky silk gown and moved with exquisite grace. Her skin was flawless, her hair as rich and silky as a black cat's fur, marked by the streak of white. Despite what Jimmy knew about her, his heart leaped, unwarranted, at her sight.

Who knew evil could be so beautiful?

The height of deceit . . .

The Orchid moved behind the seated fortune-teller, placing both hands gently on the woman's shoulders. "Actually, Madame Belinsky, from this point forward it's just us *three*. Shinji, Kento, and me. Or four, I suppose, if you count Jimmy, depending on how things turn out with him. But who knows what choices he will make? Regardless, you're no longer necessary to the team."

"But . . ." Madame Belinsky murmured.

"Oh, you *were* helpful," the Orchid interrupted. "But you're descended from a mongrel race and so you could never be considered one of us. And yet you're here . . . a witness to everything . . . so what is to be done?" The Orchid tightened her grip on the fortune teller's shoulders so that she could neither rise nor turn around.

"I helped you," Madame Belinsky said, her fake accent disappearing as her panic rose. "You promised me money. But you needn't pay, just let me go."

"Thank you for the help," the Orchid said, as she reached with one hand around the front of the woman. Jimmy hadn't noticed the Orchid's long fingernails until now. They were as sharp as razors. Literally. With a backhanded motion, fast as an adder, she slashed the fingernail of her middle finger across the throat of the fortune-teller, opening it wide. The shocked woman raised her own hand to the bleeding slash, attempting to hold the flesh together; she managed a short, anguished cry that went unheard in the din of the fireworks outside. But she could stem the tide only for a moment before the blood began gushing over her whitening hand. Her eyes widened as she realized she was coming to her end.

Jimmy tried to leap out of his chair to help.

But the Japs in black held him tight.

The fortune-teller fell face-first onto the café table, a pool of blood widening as it soaked into the velvet tablecloth.

There was nothing Jimmy could do for her.

He took a deep breath to calm himself.

He couldn't afford to panic, however gruesome the scene before him.

"She wasn't one of us," the Orchid announced calmly.

"And I am?" Jimmy asked, daring to meet her eyes.

"We'll see," she answered, wiping the blood from her middle fingernail onto the velvet tablecloth. "Your cliché-ridden philosophy leaves much to be desired. But your courage is commendable."

Jimmy's breathing steadied. He was no beginner. He had a mission to complete.

And his dying before the Orchid died wasn't part of the plan.

"You've gone to a lot of trouble for me," he said. "I'm flattered."

"You should be," she answered, smiling warmly, as if inches away there was no dead woman or widening puddle of blood.

"So?" he asked, feigning nonchalance. "Are we ever going to get down to business?"

She sighed, as if suddenly wearied from her activities. "Yes, but first I'm going to slip back through the trapdoor, returning to the catwalk beneath the pier. There it's private and quite lovely, the sheltering pier above, the rolling water alight with reflections of the moonlight below. You'll see it soon enough. We'll talk business there, Jimmy. You'll decide if you want to work with me. That is, if you want to win or lose. But first I need a moment of privacy for my meditation."

"And what am I supposed to do here with your two goons?" Jimmy asked. "Play three-handed poker with the Gypsy's tarot cards?"

She laughed. "Before we meet beneath the pier, Jimmy, my 'goons' are going to disarm you of whatever weapons you may be carrying, and then, in this little room, they will give you a taste of what happens to *anyone* who says no to me. A mere taste. Any more than that and you'd be a corpse, and what good would you be to me then?"

"Sounds fun," Jimmy said.

"I need my meditation." She looked at her henchmen. "Teach him humility. Take him to the very edge."

She walked past Jimmy without another word.

He heard the trapdoor slam shut as she descended from the shack to meditate with the ocean. And to await Jimmy's softening up. The fireworks continued outside, eliminating any chance of Jimmy calling for help. But that wasn't his style anyway. He smiled up the Jap hoodlums.

Neither smiled back.

"So this is where we get to know each other, eh Shinji?" Jimmy asked the taller of the two.

"I'm Kento," the thug replied, punching Jimmy in the face.

Jimmy saw stars.

He assessed his situation.

Being handcuffed wasn't going to make his task any easier. But they'd made the mistake of handcuffing his hands in front of his body. That meant at least one of these Japs was going to die with marks from the cuff's metal chain around his treacherous neck. As for the other . . . well, Jimmy was good at improvisation.

"You sure you wouldn't prefer we got to know each other a little better before we get . . . you know, physically involved?" Jimmy queried, unsure if the goons would get the joke.

They didn't answer.

At least, not with words.

This time, Shinji punched him in the face.

It was time Jimmy went to work.

❧

Excerpt from a letter April 23, 1943:

. . . naturally supportive of any young
man's involvement in our nation's critical
military endeavors. However, I do not think
it prudent that you enlist <u>immediately</u>,
whatever the enthusiasm currently sweeping
your internment camp. You are so close to
finishing your novel! Why invite a distraction that is literally global in scope to
interfere with your concentration? You have
already overcome the challenges of internment, grief at the loss of your father,
and the heartache of a breakup with your
girlfriend, to complete 90 percent of your
first book! Why voluntarily introduce yet
another distraction when you're so close
to completing your work and being a writer,
which was your dream? I am emphatic on this
point, Takumi, and I think by now you know
that I <u>always</u> have your best interests in
mind.
     Look, this new 442nd Division can do
without you for another month or two in a
way that Jimmy Park and the other indel-
ible characters you've created cannot. I
know you understand that. By resisting your
impulse to be among the <u>first wave</u> of volun-
teers for this new unit, you can give Jimmy
and the Orchid a life for readers. What a
gift! Not only to the readers and the nation
(your book is, after all, inspirationally
patriotic at this most critical of histor-

ical moments), but also to your deserving
characters, whom I have quite come to love.

As for your having your cake and eating
it too: I simply don't believe that you
could continue writing while in basic
training. Or that you would scrawl the con-
clusion and incorporate final revisions to
your book on a troop carrier months from
now crossing the Atlantic. Your moment as
an author is now, Takumi. Your moment as
an American soldier will come soon enough.
Please finish what you started. <u>Then</u> enlist.
Here's the truth: my marriage was perma-
nently interrupted by war; don't allow this
book, which I've come to think of as <u>ours</u>,
to suffer the same fate. Get Jimmy out of
that shack on the pier, bound as he is now
by the two Japanese thugs with brutality
on their evil minds. (Such a well written
scene—the Orchid's deadly fingernail, what
a touch!)

Your concerned partner,

Maxine

❧

THE REVISED—CHAPTER EIGHT cont'd.

In the dimness, among the countless small flashlights—one of which
Sumida had bought for two bits at a concession stand—it took longer
than he'd hoped to find the establishment of "Madame Belinsky—
Authentic Gypsy Fortune-Teller," which was not actually on the
midway but was located in a small, wooden shack halfway along the

pier. A few minutes earlier, when he was still searching the midway, a fireworks display had begun without warning over the Pike—as if the dimly lit place was not already surreal. But the fireworks confused him. In black-out conditions, what could serve as a more obvious marker to enemy aircraft than such a colorful display? At first, he could hardly believe it. Who could be behind it? But the crowd milling about the Pike responded to the impressive display almost as they would on an ordinary Fourth of July—rapt attention, oohs and ahs, and applause when a particularly big and colorful explosion rained down light over the otherwise-dimmed coast. Sure, with the first loud *boom* there'd been nervous confusion (a bomb?). But when the glorious rockets flowered red, white, and blue, people reacted to it as a rebellious display of patriotism. Perhaps that's what it was. Nonetheless, Sumida worried he might be at the center of a target for an aerial attack. No matter. He wasn't going to run away now. Didn't the government dossier that Czernicek had lifted indicate the fortune-teller's was to be the rendezvous point for a meeting between an unnamed Federal agent and the Orchid? If he was going to be bombed to oblivion trying to reach it, then so be it.

He'd seen the photograph. It was his Kyoko.

He didn't have to understand the fireworks.

And he didn't have to understand this "Orchid" business, which portrayed Kyoko as mastermind of a spy ring working to lay the groundwork for the invasion of America's West Coast by forces of the Imperial Japanese Army. Ridiculous! Kyoko was a gentle woman with little interest in politics. And anti-American espionage? She'd been valedictorian of their class at Long Beach Wilson High School, delivering a graduation speech on the blessings offered to immigrants by the American way of life. Yet the report acknowledged no such past—no past at all. Instead, it depicted her as being of unknown birthplace and upbringing, seeming to have burst into life fully realized as a femme fatale who was feared even by other brutal Japanese operatives. Sumida couldn't help but recall the Dragon Lady characters from a handful of movies he and Kyoko had walked out of because of the wearisome Oriental stereotypes. And the government report did not stop with mere insults. Seeming to take seriously the virtually impossible portrait of evil on its pages—including the absurdity of Kyoko's having committed three brutal murders (including one decapitation and dismemberment) in just the past twenty-four hours!—the report called for her assassination, to be carried out by the unnamed operative whose meeting with her had been arranged under the guise of his going over to her side.

Kyoko returned from the dead for this?

Still, Sumida was aware that since the Rialto last night nothing had remained what it had been before. His home in Echo Park was now occupied by another man. His aunt and uncle's house in South Gate was likewise occupied by strangers. His friend Tony Fortuna (now dead, apparently by Sam's own hand) hadn't recognized him. Then there was the gravesite, the newspapers, the public records. . . . So far, the only thing unchanged from what, increasingly, seemed a whole *other life*, was Czernicek, who'd confessed to being Kyoko's murderer.

The woman who was now somewhere nearby, alive.

None of it made sense. But Sumida didn't have to understand how things worked to know what he had to do.

Save his wife.

As he had failed to do before. . . .

And now he stood before the sign that read, "Madame Belinsky—Authentic Gypsy Fortune-Teller." The attraction was located in a wooden shack on the pier between a blueberry pie stand (closed for the night) and a small storefront that sold sea shells. The fireworks show continued. Sumida tried the doorknob to the tiny enterprise. It turned, unlocked. But when he pushed open the door, it jammed after just a few inches against something on the floor of the interior. He pushed harder. Still, something weighty resisted his efforts. At last, he put his shoulder to the door, leaning into it like it was a tackling sled from his freshman year of football at Wilson High. Had the crowd not been distracted by the firework show's grand finale, he surely would have had hard questions to answer and dark suspicions to assuage. ("A Jap breaking into a legitimate fortune-telling business?!") The door edged

open an inch at a time as he slowly moved whatever heavy sack of potatoes blocked the entrance inside. As the last of the fireworks exploded,
followed by a hearty round of applause from the revelers on the pier
and along the midway, Sumida managed to create an opening in the
doorway that was just wide enough for him to squeeze through. Once
inside, he closed the door so no one could follow.

Now it was pitch dark.

He illuminated the space with his pen-sized flashlight.

It had been no sack of potatoes blocking his entrance, but the
bodies of two Asian men, dressed in black, like burglars, who had
been piled one atop the other. Sumida gasped for breath. What had he
walked into? He knelt beside the men for a closer look. Their faces were
battered and bruised. Upon closer examination, not so easy in the dim
glow, he noted that their necks bore marks suggesting a narrow-gauge
length of chain had been used to strangle both. And the room smelled
of blood. Lots of it. More than the dead men's knocked-out teeth
and facial lacerations might explain. A stockyard smell. . . . Standing,
Sumida turned and wielded his light before him. That's when he saw
the Gypsy woman face down on a small velvet-covered table. The velvet
was soaked through with gore. "Madame Belinsky?" he whispered,
though he knew she wouldn't answer. He forced himself to go to her.
Gently, he lifted her head with one hand, holding the light close. Her
throat had been slit with something as sharp as a scalpel. The wound
was horrid, and he couldn't help dropping her poor head back to the
table, where it thumped on the gooey velvet.

Spade would have treated the poor woman's corpse better.

But Sumida had never seen carnage like this—never even imagined
it. In a Universal Pictures horror film the violence looked so phony that
the experience never lost its fun, whatever the monstrous plot. And
Picasso's brilliantly powerful *Guernica* mythologized violence rather
than reproducing it. But this was real. And as Sumida's adrenalin,
which had initially sustained him, began to fade, he felt sick and had to
steady himself to keep from vomiting.

What kind of sorry PI paled at violence?

Only then did he wonder: Might the killer still be here?

He removed the .38 from the back waistband of his trousers, his hand trembling. With his other hand, he moved the tiny light in a wide arc.

Aside from the corpses he was alone.

What had happened here and why?

And where was his wife?

Was one of these dead men the Federal agent? He doubted it, as the victims identical attire contradicted the plan for a solitary assailant that he'd read about in the stolen government report.

He swallowed hard. Then he almost laughed, his nerves still badly shaken. Earlier, he had thought things couldn't get worse for him. Yet now he was virtually trapped in a shack on the Long Beach pier, hundreds of Caucasians wandering outside (a quarter of them likely drunk), with three corpses here and no explanation for his presence among them that would satisfy even the most sympathetic cop or juror. (As if these days there even *were* such things as sympathetic authorities for his kind.)

The intelligence report about this being the rendezvous point for the agent and the Orchid had to have been wrong. Or perhaps the mission had been aborted due to this violence. In either case, he'd have to move the men's bodies to squeeze back out the door and distance himself from the crime scene.

He grabbed the first man by the hands and dragged him away from the door.

That's when he saw it.

A portion of the Turkish rug had been pulled up as he dragged the man across it.

Beneath, a trapdoor.

❧

Excerpt from chapter fourteen of *The Orchid and the Secret Agent*, a novel by William Thorne

Metropolitan Modern Mysteries, Inc., New York, N.Y., 1945

. . . having piled the beaten and strangled bodies of Shinji and Kento, one of whom had carried the handcuff keys in his pocket, atop one another near the front entrance, then descending through the trapdoor and down the wooden ladder, Jimmy Park stood now on the catwalk beneath the pier. The Jap heavies had been less difficult to defeat than he'd anticipated, his expert Taekwondo moves seeming new to them, which made him wonder if the pair had been intended more as a test of his skills than to actually rough him up. No matter. They were dead now. His mission prospects had improved from being seriously threatened, back when he'd had a gun held to the back of his head, to certain success, as he now saw the Orchid standing thirty yards away, leaning against the catwalk's wooden railing, her back to him and her attention seemingly focused on the moonlit, rolling breakers not far below. He could put two bullets in her from this distance, one in her head and the other through her back to her heart. But he had a few questions. And, just maybe, he wanted to see her face one more time before he ended her life.

She could not have heard his descent, as the fireworks far above the pier and the waves here below would have concealed the sound of his opening and closing the trapdoor, his feet on the wooden ladder, his cocking the gun. Nonetheless, she turned, calmly and purposefully, as if she knew just the moment he touched down on the three-foot-wide, wooden catwalk, as if she was not in the least surprised to find him unaccompanied by her goons.

Just then, the fireworks stopped.

The Pike crowd roared their appreciation for the aerial display.

Smiling, the Orchid applauded too, even as her eyes bored into his.

He was struck by the timing of the fireworks' grand finale. Suddenly, it was comparatively quiet down here, even as the ordinary sounds of the midway continued (the calliope, the roller coaster, the hum of myriad voices) and the waves rhythmically washed past the big wooden pylons. Had some invisible stage manager cued the fireworks ending, in anticipation of his leading actress's opening lines?

Indeed, the Orchid took a step toward Jimmy.

He showed the gun.

She shrugged as if it were nothing. "Do you think it is an accident that we are down here together, just the two of us? Or that you are holding a gun while I am unarmed? Do you think I would have made myself mortally vulnerable to any man, especially one who works clandestinely with the government of the United States, if I did not already know that man's mind, even if he still does not fully know it himself?"

"I know my mind," he answered, continuing slowly toward her.

She stopped, leaning against the wooden railing. "I love it down here, suspended between worlds." She looked up. "The topside of the pier above, crowded, noisy . . ." Then she looked over the side. "The dark, rolling ocean below, mysterious and unconcerned with humanity . . ." She turned back to Jimmy. "And I, suspended here on these narrow planks, between worlds, at peace in the shadows."

Jimmy wasn't taken in by her poetry. If he was distracted by anything it was by trying to figure out the engineering purpose of this catwalk, from which other wooden ladders led up to other trap doors at regular intervals for the entire length of the pier. Suspended by iron poles to the underside of the pier, the catwalk looked like it had been built long ago. Was it used for maintenance of the pylons? No matter. The Orchid had found her use: privacy among a crowd. This same privacy would serve Jimmy's purpose as well.

"You don't seem much interested in what I have to say," she observed. "So why haven't you already killed me?"

He took a few more steps toward her. "Maybe I wasn't sure I could hit you from that distance."

She scoffed. "I know how well you shoot, Jimmy. You could have put one between my eyes from twice that range."

Between the eyes. Jimmy recalled Mr. Barratt's instruction.

"Do you know the one thing I don't like about being down here?" she asked.

He said nothing, but kept his gun aimed at her head.

"It's that the swirling breezes off the water, so refreshing to exposed flesh, make it quite impossible for a girl to light a cigarette," she said.

He laughed. "Don't think I'm going to light one for you."

"Of course not, Jimmy. Besides, you probably think smoking is unhealthy, being such a straight shooter, if I may use that term colloquially even as you are actually holding a gun on me. Forgive the pun. Now, don't you want to ask me why I'd put myself in this position, why I'd risk my life on my certainty that, whatever you think now, you will shortly come over to my side?"

He waited.

She waited too, until at last: "If you want an answer, you'll have to ask," she said.

"Okay," he conceded. "Why?"

"Because you're my brother. By blood."

He hadn't expected a whopper like that. He laughed. "That's the best you can do?"

"Oh, I don't lack for imagination. I could have come up with more immediately effective arguments for your coming over to my side, Jimmy. But all those other arguments would have lacked one thing. The truth. So, in this instance, I decided to go with that."

He shook his head dismissively. "So, you're telling me you're not Japanese."

"No, I'm telling you that you *are* Japanese." She shrugged. "Well, half."

He knew the right course was to delay no longer, but to put one between her eyes. But he didn't pull the trigger, wanting to shame her first. "Go on, sister."

She shook her head. "If you're going to treat the premise as if it's a joke, I would rather you shoot me now."

"Shoot my own sister?"

"See, a joke," she snapped. "Pull the damn trigger, you son of a bitch."

He didn't.

"Go on, explain yourself," he said, wiping the sarcasm from his voice.

She folded her hands in front of her as if delivering a speech.

"You were born on February 13, 1911, in Seoul, Korea, which I don't have to tell you had been annexed the previous year by the Empire of Japan."

"Thanks for reminding me of my birthday and offering a basic history lesson."

She ignored him, continuing: "Your mother, Kyung-Sun, and your father, Seung, left Korea without proper Japanese authorization sixteen months later, arriving on these shores and calling upon connections to gain entrance. Here, you became a veritable Andy Hardy, All-American. But have you ever wondered why your parents went to such ends to escape their homeland."

"Jap occupation, for one," he answered. "And the promise of America for another."

She sighed. "I'm sorry to tell you that your mother was assaulted in the first months of the occupation by a Japanese soldier named Himura, which means 'Scarlet Village,' resulting in her pregnancy with you. Your adopted, Korean 'father' did the honorable thing of marrying Kyung-Sun despite her disgrace. He gave you his name. But you are no Park. You are a Himura, like me. Yes, the soldier was my father. I am not proud of his actions. They were dishonorable. But I am here to make amends with you by welcoming you into your true family as if you were not half-mongrel. No one ever need know. And, together, we will do great things."

"That's quite a story."

She nodded. "We'll bring honor to our ancestors."

He stepped closer, having heard enough. "Where you go wrong, my lovely and deadly Orchid, is that I am color-blind, which is an inherited trait. No one in my mother's family suffers from this minor impairment. But my father, Seung Park, is also color-blind. So, you see, he *is* my true father, in every way. My color blindness is a personal detail I don't advertise. Still, you've been misinformed. Your researchers dropped the ball, if you'll forgive an Americanism."

Her eyes widened in surprise at this turn.

He raised the gun to her forehead. "Give a girl enough rope . . . You have made your final mistake, sister."

❧

Excerpt from a letter May 25, 1943:

. . . and so, while I appreciate the dramatic ambiguity created by Jimmy's color-
blindness being a brilliant fabrication on
his part, such a ruse nonetheless has the
effect of allowing for the possibility that
he actually <u>might</u> <u>be</u> her half-brother, and
I fear we mustn't indulge the idea that our
hero may be half-Japanese. So let's stream-
line the scene and make his color-blindness
simply true rather than a ruse, removing
all doubt and thereby trapping the conniving
Orchid in an unequivocal lie. I love that!
Happy note: at the editorial meeting,
my colleagues rallied behind the idea that
the Orchid has "the potential" to drive an
entire series, even as a villain, much as
Dr. Fu Manchu has made a boatload of money
for author and publisher. Of course, this
would depend on the sales of the first book,
and so at this time we can't offer you a
contract for a sequel or subsequent titles
in a series. But the prospects are good.
Isn't it exciting news, Takumi! Particularly as you'd expressed some hesitation at
actually killing off the Orchid. (I think
your commercial radar was working in ways
you may not even have recognized!)
In any case, we still need to provide
a satisfying climax to <u>The Orchid and the</u>
<u>Secret Agent</u>. After all, Jimmy Park can't
simply be defeated at the end. But that's

where the Orchid's ominous bodyguard comes in—the Phantom. Look, with your enlistment coming up in less than a month, and the actual, contracted deadline for the completed draft on the heels of that, I don't think there's time to go back and establish rich character details for the Phantom without dislodging the house of cards we've constructed. However, the more I think about it, the more I think his being a mysterious figure right up to the end, when his appearance is revealed, against type, to be that of an "ordinary" man, is quite effective. Perhaps as foreshadowing you could put something in earlier about the Phantom's presumed "man on the street" appearance. Maybe in one of Jimmy's conversations with Mr. Barratt . . . And _if_ this proves to be the first book in a series about the duel between Jimmy and the Orchid, then our hero's elimination of her top bodyguard will be, I think, a sufficient and satisfying climax for book #1. Anyway, I know you'll figure something out, as you always do!

Regardless, there's no time left for dilly-dallying at Manzanar. (As there surely won't be any time at the basic training camp they'll soon be shipping you off to in Mississippi, or wherever you said it was.) So get to it, my talented, and perhaps soon-to-be-famous, author!

Yours Thrilled,

Maxine

THE REVISED—CHAPTER EIGHT cont'd.

Sumida poked his head down through the open trapdoor before descending the ladder. It was a good thing he did, as he saw what was happening below and could react accordingly. On a narrow wooden catwalk, suspended ten feet above the surface of the ocean by metal poles attached to the underside of the pier, a man held a gun on a woman. They stood thirty or forty yards from the base of the ladder. The silhouetted man had his back to Sumida. The woman leaned with unexpected languor against the wooden railing—as if she was not even being held at gunpoint. Such *sangfroid*! Strange, Sumida thought, as his Kyoko was more the nervous type. The two talked, though Sumida could not make out their words. Then clouds parted, or perhaps it was the clearing of the smoke from the fireworks, and now the moonlight reflected off the water. He got a better look at the woman. Her silhouette, slinky in a satin gown, brought to mind Kyoko's beautiful body, which he had cherished from the moment they'd become clumsy but passionate lovers as seniors in high school. And as his eyes further adjusted to the light he made out the features of her face.

The light still wasn't ideal.

At this distance, it was difficult to discern details.

Sumida's mind was clouded from the past twenty-four hours.

All reasons to doubt what he saw ... but he had no doubt. It was Kyoko. Somehow, she was alive.

He hesitated no longer, but closed the trapdoor quietly behind him and stealthily started down the ladder. He knew Kyoko could see his descent. But she didn't give him up to the man with the gun. Instead, she kept talking, maybe stalling for time to allow Sumida to get into position.

He was, after all, her best hope.

Who was the man with the gun and why was he holding Kyoko at bay? It didn't matter.

At the foot of the ladder, Sumida considered his options. He could call out to the armed man, demanding that he drop his weapon, as they did in the movies. But this wasn't the movies. And Sumida was no gun-slinger. He didn't relish any Western-style showdown, wherein the man would turn and they both would fire. Sumida didn't like his odds in such a confrontation. Another option was to creep forward along the wooden catwalk until he was close enough to put the gun to the back of the man's head, whereupon his demand to "drop it" could not be resisted. But he feared that even with the sound of the water below and the amusement park sounds above, he could not be silent enough to draw *that* close. Besides, his movement along the creaking catwalk would inevitably cause enough sway (even if only a little) that the man would feel Sumida's approach before he arrived.

The third option was to fire from here.

It wasn't so far. He could steady himself against the base of the ladder, using two hands on the pistol. Perhaps he hadn't thought of himself as being a man who'd shoot another man in the back. But that was more movie-think. Besides *this* man was holding a gun on Kyoko! Mustn't it have been like this before, when Czernicek had held a pistol on Kyoko at the edge of the water someplace along the LA harbor, not so far from here? That *had* happened. He'd identified the body. He was not a madman. Yet here he was. He felt his heart begin to race.

He mustn't let his adrenalin interfere with the precision of his shot.

And he mustn't wait so long that the conversation at the far end of the catwalk ended with the man's shooting Kyoko.

He put both hands on the gun, aimed, and fired.

❧

Excerpt from chapter fourteen, con't. of *The Orchid and the Secret Agent*, a novel by William Thorne

Metropolitan Modern Mysteries, Inc., New York, N.Y., 1945

. . . But just before he pulled the trigger to eliminate the Orchid for good, Jimmy felt a hard blow to the back of his left shoulder, spinning him around and almost knocking the gun from his right hand. His first thought was of the Orchid, who, being so close, might move in on him with razor sharp precision now that he was disoriented; his second thought was that she'd have no time to reach him, as the momentum of the blow was hurtling him, helplessly, over the railing and into the ocean; his third thought was that he'd been shot; his fourth was to look in the direction from which the shot had come; his fifth was that he saw the shooter standing at the foot of the ladder, gun still raised; his sixth was that the shooter, who must be the Phantom, looked just as ordinary as Mr. Barratt had predicted; his seventh thought was to aim at the Phantom and to fire (action and thought being one now), even as Jimmy was going backward over the side of the catwalk; his eighth was that he had indeed hit his assailant in the gut (likely putting an end to the second-most-dangerous Jap on the West Coast); his ninth was subsumed by the cold splash of the water, into which he sunk like a stone; his tenth was that he had to rise to the surface and swim back to shore, despite the ache in his left shoulder, in order to survive to fight another day. All this in a matter of two or three seconds, plenty of time for a whole life to unspool, like a film ratcheting off a reel and turning a lucid story on a movie screen to meaningless white.

Jimmy Park would not settle for mere white.

He burst the surface of the salty, rolling sea and saw the Orchid on the catwalk above him approaching the gunman, who had collapsed, wounded, into an awkward sitting position at the base of the ladder. Jimmy believed he could still hit her from here, even as he bobbed in the water. He was that good a shot. But in his fall he had dropped his .45, which was likely settling on the sandy floor of the ocean right about now. So he ducked his head under the surface to avoid the evil pair's notice and started swimming for the shore, pulling himself forward with his right arm only, as by now his left arm had gone numb and useless.

THE REVISED—CHAPTER EIGHT cont'd.

Sitting on the wooden catwalk, supported by the ladder at his back, bleeding from a hole in his left side just under his rib cage, Sumida tried to return his gun to the back waistband of his trousers, but it fell from his hand. The gut shot hurt. He watched the woman approach. He noted her walk—all sensuality and aggression, like a leopard—and he realized that this was not the Kyoko he had known, loved, married, and lost, however familiar her appearance. Yes, she had the same sparkling eyes ... but this woman bore an expression of barely restrained, malicious power, which he had never seen in his wife, who had been many things (not all of them good) but never this. So who was this? The cartoonish villainess in the government report—the Orchid?

But she asked first, as she drew near. "Who are you?"

"I was your husband," he answered.

"What?" There was menace in her voice, despite his having just saved her life. Clearly, she did not like being confused. And, if the government report was true, then she was capable of exerting lethal force. He couldn't afford to die now. Not with this excursion a bust (involving this *other* Kyoko), while Czernicek, the killer of his *real* wife, remained alive still in the hotel room.

"I've taken no husband," she said.

"I'm speaking of another life," he answered, as rationally as possible. Talking was difficult, his midsection feeling aflame, but he had things to say. "You were someone else. Identical in appearance, but different ... Don't ask me to explain, because I can't."

"Do you work for the United States government?" she asked.

"No."

Standing over him, she shook her head. "Maybe you're just a mad dog looking to be put out of his misery."

Maybe he was, he thought. But not quite yet.

"In any case, I should thank you for your well-timed shot," she said. "What is your name?"

"Satoki Samuel Sumida. My friends call me Sam." Bleeding, he hadn't time to introduce further facts that would only compel from her more questions—especially since he had a few questions of his own. "Who did I shoot?"

"The man you shot was nothing," she answered.

He had to strain his neck and shoulders to look up, his midsection offering no support. "No, *I* am nothing," he said. "Just ask almost anyone."

She knelt beside him, pushing aside his suit coat to see his bloodied shirt. "You're delirious."

"I wish that were so."

Now that she was just inches away from him, he caught her scent. It was *Lucien Lelong* perfume. Familiar, of course. For a moment, he looked only at the side of her face, allowing himself to imagine that this was his Kyoko. From so close, there was no distinction, mannerisms melting away. He had never thought he'd experience his wife's physical presence again. Yet here she was, now. His heart swelled, and he wished he could say how sorry he was for the ways he had failed her, his vain and distracted nature. He wished too that he could tell her he forgave her betrayal, which he believed was more about their strained marriage than about her true character. If he was going to die here beneath the pier, what better final image to take with him? With the back of his right hand he gently touched the perfect cheek, scented of *Lucien Lelong* . . .

The woman snapped back, as if revolted by his touch.

His reverie ceased, its sudden absence hitting him almost as hard as the bullet.

Of course this was not his wife.

This was the traitorous criminal described in the government report. (Assuming the Federal agents had gotten it right, which they usually did, though in this case the violence and manner of her alleged crimes strained belief, seeming the stuff of Saturday matinee B-pictures or pulp spy novels.) Indeed, it had been the seemingly exaggerated nature of her criminality that had encouraged Sam to ignore the report itself (clearly not *his* Kyoko) when Czernicek first provided it and to put all his faith in the attached photograph instead. So he'd been taken in, as the photograph failed to convey the otherness of this woman who bore Kyoko's face—the Orchid—the otherness of her walk, her facial expressions, her way of speech. What it all amounted to was yet another question: should he shoot her now himself, thereby removing a national security threat? Subsequent questions followed. Could he even reach the gun where he'd dropped it on the catwalk? Likely not ... but was that a good enough reason not to try? He was an American and had responsibilities. Or was the entire report of her venality mere exaggerated racial prejudice? And, in either case, what of Czernicek, the killer of his real wife?

"I have a motorboat and men coming any second and cars waiting on the shore," she said, standing and stepping away from him. He noticed how sharp her fingernails looked. "I can instruct my men to drop you at the hospital," she continued. "Otherwise, you will bleed to death. I can't say if any of your vital organs have been hit. So you may bleed to death anyway. Regardless, honor dictates that I make such an offer since you saved my life. Even if you are a madman."

He considered his options.

Clearly, he could never climb up the ladder. Nor could he drop into the ocean and swim to shore. And even if he could do either, how would he get a cab ride back to the Barclay Hotel, a "Jap" soaked from the ocean and bleeding from a gunshot wound? No, she was offering him his only way back to Czernicek. His only chance to make good on the vengeance he'd sworn in that other world, his world.

"I accept your offer," he said.

She picked up his gun and handed it back to him.

About then, he heard the sound of a motorboat approaching.

❧

Excerpt from chapter fifteen of *The Orchid and the Secret Agent*, a novel by William Thorne
     Metropolitan Modern Mysteries, Inc., New York, N.Y., 1945

... but, fortunately, Jimmy Park had always been an outstanding swimmer, having won ribbons and medals on his Glendale High

School team. He made it to shore, where he took stock of his injury. The bullet had passed clean through his shoulder, missing the brachial artery, so he tore a strip of linen from his soaked shirt, wrapped the strip around his shoulder covering the entrance and exit wounds, and made his way up from the sand to the midway. There, in no time, the wet, disheveled appearance of a bleeding Oriental drew the attention of the police. With his good arm, Jimmy showed them his soggy but still legible special ID, and within moments an ambulance arrived to take him to safety.

The doctor told him he'd been very lucky.

Maybe so, but he didn't feel lucky. Nor did he feel he even deserved good luck, having allowed his verbal parrying with the Orchid to cost him his mission. How many thousands of lives were now jeopardized by her escape? Why hadn't he just put one between her eyes, as Mr. Barratt had instructed? He didn't like to admit that her female wiles had had something to do with it. His nation was at war and a man couldn't afford to be soft, even where women were concerned. Jimmy had never felt so disconsolate, so ashamed.

Admitted to a private hospital room on the fifth floor of County General, where the best gunshot men had cleaned and stabilized his wound, Jimmy passed on the painkilling pills that the nurse offered.

"Tough guy, huh?" said Mr. Barratt, who entered the room just as the nurse was leaving.

"I deserve whatever pain I'm feeling," Jimmy said listlessly. "It serves to remind me of my failure and to inspire me to give no quarter if I should ever be granted another chance to finish off that sorceress of violence."

Mr. Barratt laughed. "Quite a speech, Jimmy. But you've got it wrong."

"What?"

"Well, it's true you missed an opportunity with the Orchid, but it looks likely you got the Phantom, which deals a vicious blow to her organization."

Jimmy nodded, unimpressed. In the seconds falling backward from the catwalk, just before he'd hit the water, he'd seen the deceptively

ordinary-looking Jap go down in a heap, gutshot. From a marksman-
ship perspective it had been a whale of a shot. But this was no shooting
contest, no gentlemen's pastime. The better shot would have been the
point-blank bullet for the Orchid.

"The elimination of the Orchid's right-hand man is an important
victory for our nation, Jimmy," Mr. Barratt continued. "Our first clean
win in the intelligence war."

Jimmy merely shrugged. "Maybe if we'd been able to take him
alive," he muttered. "At least then we'd have been able to get some information out of him to help dismantle their wretched organization."

Mr. Barratt beamed. "We might just have that opportunity."

"What?" Jimmy asked, sitting up straighter in the hospital bed.
The self-recrimination stopped in favor of the renewed enthusiasm of
a patriot.

Mr. Barratt turned and started for the wooden wardrobe in a
corner of the private room. He opened the doors and removed Jimmy's
still-damp suit from its hanger, tossing it onto the hospital bed. "Get
dressed," he instructed.

Jimmy picked up his suit jacket, which had a hole through the
front and back of the left shoulder.

"I didn't have time to stop by your place for a change of clothes,"
Mr. Barratt said. "A little dampness won't kill you."

Jimmy slid his legs around and stood up slightly unsteadily from
the bed. "What's happened?" he asked, tucking his hospital gown like a
long, wrinkled shirt inside his moist trousers.

"We've intercepted a call from a downtown hotel reporting that a
gut-shot Jap stumbled into their lobby a few minutes ago, brandishing
a handgun. He made his way upstairs to a room rented earlier to a Mr.
Henry Czernicek, a name that in the past fifteen minutes I've learned
via hotline from our people in DC does not exist on any tax records,
census, or immigration reports."

"So the police are moving in?" Jimmy asked, sitting on the chair in
the corner of the room to put his wet socks on his feet, his Florsheims
at arm's reach.

"No."

"What? Why not? We can't let him get away. It's got to be the Phantom."

Mr. Barratt nodded. "You've answered your own question, Jimmy. We don't want the police getting to the Phantom first. If so, he'll be booked, jailed, arraigned, tried, convicted, executed, etcetera. From a law-enforcement standpoint it'll go fine. But from an intelligence-gathering viewpoint, it's inefficient. You understand that there are methods of persuasion that *we* might execute that are unavailable to ordinary law enforcement and judicial agencies, right?"

Jimmy understood. He finished tying his shoes. (Not so easy with a bum shoulder.) He stood. "Can you help me with this jacket?" he asked, indicating his wounded left shoulder.

Mr. Barratt nodded and helped his agent into the dank suit jacket. "I'm only too happy to be your valet, Mr. Park," he said kiddingly. "Just so long as you don't call me your 'houseboy.'"

"You're going to have to be my chauffeur, too," Jimmy added.

"Let's go."

"Wait," Jimmy said. "I don't have a gun."

"You shoot with your right hand, right?"

"Yeah, the wound is no problem."

Mr. Barratt reached inside his suit coat and withdrew from his own shoulder holster his standard-issue weapon, which he handed to Jimmy. "You're a better shot than I am."

Jimmy didn't bother with false modesty. There wasn't time.

He just took the gun.

Turning to leave, the two men were stopped by a skinny, five-foot-tall nurse standing in the doorway.

"He can't go," she said. "He's not discharged."

Mr. Barratt showed her his ID. "Maybe just this once you could make an exception, ma'am."

THE REVISED—CHAPTER NINE

Two worlds, like audiences, disperse
And leave the soul alone.

—Emily Dickinson

Sumida's squeaking left shoe was heavy with blood, which still flowed down his side. The Florsheim left a print with every step he took along the fifth-floor hallway from the elevator to Czernicek's hotel room. If he had entertained any notion of evading pursuit—from the police, pro-Japanese Fifth Columnists, Federal agents, whomever—the bloody footprints would have given him away. But he harbored no such notions. He'd already lost too much blood for pulp fiction fantasies of escape. His ears rang, his eyesight wavered, his breaths came fast and short, his body temperature felt arctic—he knew he hadn't much time. Besides, he'd wearied of hiding from authorities (the absurd night spent sleeping in the stolen Chrysler Royale . . .), just as he'd wearied of being in this world that was not his any longer.

He didn't require much time to do what was left for him to do anyway.

He opened the door to the hotel room and, hoping to make a dignified entrance, stumbled inside.

Czernicek was where Sumida had left him, still gagged and handcuffed to the radiator. The police detective had regained consciousness, though he looked nearly as unsteady sitting upright as Sumida felt walking. Nonetheless, Czernicek's eyes burned with fury, his face streaked with blood from the kick Sumida had administered before he'd left for the Pike—a lifetime ago.

Sumida pulled the hand towel from Czernicek's mouth.

The police detective spit at Sumida, but missed.

Sumida paid the gesture no heed, managing to make it to a chair that faced his quarry from six-feet distant. He took the gun from the waistband of his trousers and aimed it at Czernicek's heart.

"You're going to shoot an LAPD detective, Sumida?"

Sumida laughed. The notion of his being kept from doing what needed to be done merely because of a man's job title struck him as hilarious.

The problem was that it hurt too much to laugh.

So he stopped laughing.

"You're making a big mistake," Czernicek said.

"It wasn't her," Sumida said.

"Let me go, you son of a bitch, or I swear you'll pay," Czernicek snapped.

"What are you going to do, kill me?" Sumida asked, again having to fight off laughter.

"I'll tear you a new asshole."

"I quiver in fear, Czernicek."

"All I got to do is yell for help and the hotel dick'll be here in . . ."

"You raise your voice and I'll give you a bullet all the sooner," Sumida interrupted.

Sumida watched Czernicek's eyes move from the bloody shoe up his left side, which was soaked all the way to the rib cage. Sumida could smell the reek of his own blood. But the cop pretended not to notice, perhaps hoping Sumida would lose consciousness before taking his revenge. Sumida would allow no such moment for hope to alight in Czernicek's blue eyes. "Yeah, Mr. LAPD detective, I'm shot, so very shortly we're going to be dying here together."

The cop said nothing.

"Did you hear me tell you that the woman wasn't Kyoko?" Sumida asked.

"But I saw the picture," Czernicek answered, softening his tone to one of rationality—a truly desperate maneuver for a man of his ilk.

Sumida shrugged. "A kind of twin, I guess. I don't know. But she wasn't my wife. More like her opposite, actually. Tough as nails. Queen bitch. But she did me a good turn after I saved her life."

"What'd she do?"

"She got me here in time to finish you."

"But it had to be your Kyoko," Czernicek insisted. "Maybe she's changed a little. But it had to be her!"

Sumida sighed. "Let's face it, Czernicek, when you kill a woman she doesn't come back."

"But with so many strange things going on lately..." Czernicek started.

"She never comes back," Sumida interrupted, cocking the gun.

"How can you make a moral decision in a world you don't even understand, Sumida?"

"Understand?" Sumida felt the life slipping from him, his heartbeat wavering, his head pounding, his vision going... "I didn't understand the world even *before* last night. I don't think the world is ever something you can understand, even when it seems ordinary. So all you can do is try to figure out what you've been put here to do. And then do it."

"And what were you put here to do, Sumida? Commit murder? Kill a bound man in a hotel room?"

"Avenge the killing of the woman who loved me."

"She *didn't* love you, Sumida. Get it straight and you'll get it right!"

Sumida hesitated. "Okay, I'll take your word for it, Czernicek. I'll amend what I said. I'm here to avenge the killing of the woman who didn't love me." Sumida extended the gun and slipped his finger onto the trigger. "The point is I loved her."

"Please don't, Sam," Czernicek begged. "We're partners in this goddamn crazy world!"

Sumida shook his head. "You'll kill again if I don't take care of business." By nature, Sumida was no executioner. He was hardly even a man of action. But this was a duty. "*Shikata ga nai,*" he muttered. *This cannot be helped.*

"What the hell's that mean?" Czernicek demanded.

Sumida didn't answer. With the last of his strength, he held his arm ramrod straight, keeping the gun pointed at his target. He pulled the trigger. The last thing he felt before losing consciousness was the weapon's kick, the last sound its explosive discharge.

THE END

Begun: Camp Shelby, Hattiesburg, Mississippi, July 5, 1943
Completed: Cecina, Italy, July 3, 1944

❧

Excerpt from the final chapter of *The Orchid and the Secret Agent*, a novel by William Thorne
    Metropolitan Modern Mysteries, Inc., New York, N.Y., 1945

Jimmy Park and Mr. Barratt pressed through the bathrobe-attired hotel guests who'd recklessly begun milling in the fifth-floor hallway just a few moments after the sound of the gunshot. Being the first authorities on the scene, Barratt and Park ordered the guests back to their rooms. (The two had been in the lobby at the time of the shot and had sprinted up the five flights.) Now, Mr. Barratt prepared to kick down the door to the corner room, registered to a Henry Czernicek. Jimmy stood at his side, the handgun drawn and ready.

"Try the knob," Jimmy whispered. "Maybe it's unlocked."

"I kind of like kicking in doors," Mr. Barratt whispered in return.

"Then have at it, sir," Jimmy said.

Mr. Barratt kicked the door in.

Jimmy rushed inside, the gun held before him. "Federal agents, nobody move!" he shouted.

But nobody was going to be moving in that room.

Mr. Barratt checked the bathroom. "Clear," he said.

Jimmy put the gun away and indicated with a nod of his head the body of an Oriental man, bloodied down his entire left side, slumped in a chair. A handgun rested on the rug beside him, beneath where his right hand dangled. "That's him," Jimmy said. "The one I shot under the pier—the Phantom."

Mr. Barratt nodded, then turned. "So who's this one?"

Handcuffed to the radiator in a seated position was a tall Caucasian man who leaned against the wall, lifeless, his eyes wide. There was a small black hole in the center of his chest and a large splash of blood on the wall at his back and in a pool on the rug around him.

Jimmy turned back toward the Phantom. "What's the connection between these two?"

Mr. Barratt had no answer.

"Was the white guy an enemy of the Phantom or a co-conspirator who'd failed some kind of assignment?" Jimmy mused aloud. "And why did the Phantom come straight here instead of getting medical attention? What was so pressing that he'd sacrifice his own life to take this guy out?"

Again, Mr. Barratt merely shook his head. "The cops will be here any minute." He removed two fingerprint kits from his suit-coat pocket and tossed one to Jimmy. "We need prints before the LAPD arrives and starts in with their usual messy bullying."

Jimmy knelt beside the Phantom, who looked as ordinary as the Jap clerk at his local bakery. He opened the inkpad and removed the card stock sheet, which was divided into ten squares for each of the fingers. Next, taking the dead man's cold hand, he pressed the thumb into the ink and then moved the thumb over to the card—to his surprise, where a fingerprint ought to have been was a black sphere, no distinctive lines at all. He tried it again with the index finger. Same result. Confused, he looked at the Phantom's hand. There were no swirling prints on any of the fingers. And the same was true for the left hand as well. "What the heck?" he muttered.

Mr. Barratt looked at Jimmy with the same confused expression.

The Caucasian likewise had no fingerprints.

"Who are these guys?" Jimmy inquired.

"I don't like it," Mr. Barratt said.

"Is it possible to have your fingerprints shaved or burned clean off?" Jimmy asked.

"These Jap agents will do anything," Mr. Barratt answered. "That's what makes them so dangerous."

"Hardly human without a fingerprint," Jimmy mused.

"That's not the only way these enemies are inhuman," Mr. Barratt said. "Every breath they take is different from us."

Jimmy wanted to agree, but dead bodies, even those of one's enemies, always looked human. As if death restored to them what their corrupt lives seemed to have taken forever. Jimmy wanted to feel good about the accomplishments of the past hours: the killing of the Phantom and, perhaps of equal importance, the discovery of this dead Caucasian, whose absent fingerprints suggested dark, co-conspiratorial involvement with the Jap spies. Sure, the Orchid had escaped, but now she was on the run. Her capture or killing was only a matter of time, Jimmy believed. Yet there was something about these bodies that shook him in ways that even far more grotesque murder scenes had not. He caught himself; he couldn't afford to go soft now. Not with America at stake.

"This is just the beginning, Jimmy," Mr. Barratt said.

Jimmy nodded. "I'm in for the duration," he answered. "You can count on that, sir."

Mr. Barratt smiled. "I know that, Jimmy."

Six LAPD cops busted into the room like a battalion of circus clowns. What they'd make of the missing fingerprints was anybody's guess. Jimmy and Mr. Barratt wouldn't be around to observe. Showing the police their IDs they departed the room, crossed the hallway to the elevator, and made their way to the ground floor.

They still had much to do to make the country safe.

THE END

Maxine Wakefield
Associate Editor
Metropolitan Modern Mysteries, Inc.
243 W. 54th St.
New York, N.Y.

August 23, 1944

Mrs. Ayako Sato
Manzanar War Relocation Ctr.
Block 14-1-3
Manzanar, Cal.

My dear Mrs. Sato,

First, allow me to express my heartfelt
sympathies for the recent loss of your
brilliant son Takumi. I had the pleasure of
working closely with him in the year and a
half before he volunteered for the US Army,
where he truly distinguished himself above
and beyond the call of duty. The posthumous
awarding of the Silver Star for his actions
in Cecina, Italy, attests to his courage
and willingness for self-sacrifice. You must
be so proud of your son.

As you know, the novel that Takumi completed in draft before his induction, The
Orchid and the Secret Agent, is now due for
publication in February of next year. Paper
shortages and severe understaffing in our
production department delayed the book's
original release date. However, that delay
may serve the book's interests. Since your
son's recent military honors we've concluded that, even though the contract calls

for publication to be under the pen name
of William Thorne, the novel now may carry
more weight in the marketplace coming from
a Nisei war hero. I know how hard Takumi
worked on this book and that he'd come to
consider it very seriously. (In one of his
last letters to me, written on a troop ship
crossing the Atlantic, he indicated that he
was writing a kind of companion piece that
he said might not be to my taste but was of
the utmost importance to him—what clearer
sign that The Orchid and the Secret Agent
was close to his heart?)

As his heir, any changes to the contracted
publication of the book (the author's name,
specifically) must be approved by you, Mrs.
Sato. I will need you to sign and return
the enclosed release form. You needn't have
it notarized, but can merely sign it and
pop it in the enclosed stamped envelope to
get it right back to us. Many thanks for
your support!

Speaking personally, I have until now
been spared the loss of anyone close to
me in this war, having always been single
and somewhat married to my work, and, so,
losing Takumi early last month felt to me
like losing family. I believe we honor his
memory by putting his name on his work and,
if the book sells well, perhaps we can hire
ghostwriters to continue the saga of secret
agent Jimmy Park, perpetuating in subsequent exciting titles (that pesky Orchid is
still out there) the name of author Takumi
Sato!

Once more, thank you in advance for your
quick action regarding the enclosed legal

document. And please accept my compas-
sionate prayers at this tragic time.

Yours,

Maxine Wakefield
Maxine Wakefield,
Associate Editor,
Metropolitan Modern Mysteries, Inc.

Post Script

*A*mong *the collected papers of the pioneering female mystery book editor Maxine Wakefield, who retired from publishing in 1971 and died of an aneurism in 1981, is a page torn from what appears to have been a school composition book. The page is filed along with marketing correspondence, reviews, and press clippings related to* The Orchid and the Secret Agent. *The lined sheet bears just two sentences, in careful handwriting, "My son made his feelings clear to me in his letters home these past months. Therefore, my answer to your request, Miss Wakefield, is no." The sheet is signed and dated, "Ayako Sato, August 31, 1944."*

The Orchid and the Secret Agent *by William Thorne was published in February 1945. It sold well, but never spawned a sequel, likely due to Mrs. Sato's belief that her son had already written the only "sequel" he would ever have cared to provide,* The Revised, *which had been delivered from Italy to the Manzanar Relocation Camp along with the rest of Pfc. Sato's modest soldier's belongings. Sato seems to have structured the story to wrap through and around* The Orchid and the Secret Agent *like a snake navigating a trellis. Owing to its occasional use of what was then considered "profane" language, the handwritten manuscript was likely not intended for publication and, apparently, was never forwarded to Miss Wakefield or any other publishers.*

The family of Takumi Sato had his remains interred in the Japanese section of the Evergreen Cemetery in Los Angeles, beside his father's grave. The location is not far from where Takumi's most accomplished (if heretofore unpublished) character, Satoki Samuel Sumida, failed to find his wife's final resting place.

About the Author

Gordon McAlpine is the author of the critically acclaimed novel, *Hammett Unwritten*. He is also the author of three previous novels and has been described by *Publisher's Weekly* as "a gifted stylist, with clean, clear and muscular prose." Additionally, he has co-written a nonfiction book called *The Way of Baseball: Finding Stillness at 95 MPH* and is the author of a popular trilogy of novels for middle-grade readers, The Misadventures of Edgar and Allan Poe. He has published fiction and book reviews in journals and anthologies both in the United States and abroad. He lives with his wife, Julie, in southern California.